TO C
and

FURTHER
UP THE BEACH

DAVID MONK

authorHOUSE

AuthorHouse™ UK
1663 Liberty Drive
Bloomington, IN 47403 USA
www.authorhouse.co.uk
Phone: 0800 047 8203 (Domestic TFN)
+44 1908 723714 (International)

© 2019 David Monk. All rights reserved.

No part of this book may be reproduced, stored in a retrieval system, or transmitted by any means without the written permission of the author.

Published by AuthorHouse 01/17/2020

ISBN: 978-1-5462-9387-3 (sc)
ISBN: 978-1-5462-9386-6 (e)

Print information available on the last page.

Any people depicted in stock imagery provided by Getty Images are models, and such images are being used for illustrative purposes only. Certain stock imagery © Getty Images.

This book is printed on acid-free paper.

Because of the dynamic nature of the Internet, any web addresses or links contained in this book may have changed since publication and may no longer be valid. The views expressed in this work are solely those of the author and do not necessarily reflect the views of the publisher, and the publisher hereby disclaims any responsibility for them.

To my wonderful wife, Caroline, and my beloved sons, Simon and Thomas.

I have long been fascinated about the people we are but do not allow others to see.

Personal experience, as well as a long career as a social worker with troubled children, has taught me that young people often suffer major problems accessing and articulating painful feelings related to their childhood. This is particularly true for boys and young men. It frequently has a profoundly negative impact on their later emotional and mental health, as well as their happiness and that of those around them.

I passionately believe, therefore, that one of the greatest gifts we can offer children and young people to help them navigate the complexities of childhood and adolescence is well-judged and genuine enquiry as to how they are feeling, plus, of course, the time to listen. This should most certainly not simply be the preserve of social workers or others in the helping professions.

Further Up the Beach started its journey as an autobiographical account, but made the transition into fiction principally because, through the process of writing, I found elements of fiction creeping into the narrative to the extent that I could no longer reasonably lay claim to the label of autobiography.

Although inevitably my own experiences have shaped the nature of Sam's narrative, the final result does not therefore set out to be an account of any particular individual, nor even an amalgam of individuals. All characters are fictitious, as are the events described. The choice of Lincolnshire for Sam's home has no particular significance, although I have deliberately chosen a location some way from the south of England, which is important for the purposes of Sam's story.

I also chose to retain the idea of setting the scene in the era in which I grew up because that was when I knew most about being a child. This was a period in which the divide between generations was frequently dramatic, owing to the aftermath of the war and the flowering of a new and highly challenging youth culture.

Two particular books have also inspired me to write *Further Up the Beach*. The first is Charles Dickens' masterful portrayal of the influence of one generation on its successor in *Hard Times*. The second is a brilliant textbook for those working with young people, called *Teens Who Hurt* by Kenneth V. Hardy and Tracey A. Laszloffy, with its highly illuminating and readable analysis of trauma amongst young people.

Sam's tale is about the children in the world who may have untold feelings and worries they crave to tell, but dare not. It is also for the adults who now carry the privilege and responsibility of nurturing the next generation, but who may remain imprisoned by the frightening or shameful feelings they have been unable to shed since childhood.

ACKNOWLEDGEMENTS

Huge and grateful thanks to dear Caroline for her support and endless fortitude as I have pored over successive drafts of *Further Up the Beach*. I have also very much appreciated close friends and family looking over earlier, much less polished drafts, which was very helpful to me in developing this final published version.

I would like to thank Nicki Copeland, my copy-editor, for her professionalism and patience, as well as Cecelia John, my smart and eagle-eyed proofreader.

I am greatly indebted to Susan Wax, psychoanalyst. Sam's tale could never have been told without all that Susan has taught me about the workings of the human mind in general, and my own in particular.

I hope that *Further Up the Beach* will be of interest to anyone who, like me, is curious about families, human behaviour and the people we really are.

'We wear the mask that grins and lies
It hides our cheeks and shades our eyes,-
This debt we pay to human guile;
With torn and bleeding hearts we smile….'
Paul Laurence Dunbar (1872–1906)

CONTENTS

1. Burning Embers 1
2. Grand Theft 9
3. Red Ants And All That 17
4. D Day 25
5. Further Up The Beach...35
6. Bath Time 47
7. Garage Talk.. 57
8. Up High (1)..61
9. I Promise To Do My Best...................................... 69
10. Rescue 73
11. Two Wheels... 79
12. A Little Snip 85
13. The Rot 89
14. Another Planet 99
15. Southbound.. 111
16. Up High (2) 121
17. Love And Affection 129
18. I Believe In You..137
19. On Probation 145
20. Boomerang..155
21. Sea Bed.. 161
22. Epilogue 175

1. BURNING EMBERS

Sam knows in his heart of hearts that his father is dying when, just after Christmas, he takes to his bed and spends more time there than anywhere else. This is well over a decade after the massive coronary which nearly sees Walter off on the first day of spring, so Sam can already hear people saying that, all things considered, his father has done very well. He has, of course, but on the other hand, he is still only in his sixties and so is not at all old.

Sam becomes even more convinced that Walter is near the end of his life when he and his wife, as two young parents, sit in the large square garden of his parents' detached house and squeal with delight as their tiny young son takes his first steps between their adoring outstretched arms.

As the proud new father looks up, he sees his own father framed in the bedroom dormer window with a wistful smile on his face. He seems to know too that his time is nearly over. On the other hand, that of Sam and Chloe, his wife, is poised at some uncertain early or mid-point, even though they do not think about that; that of Barnaby, their heroic tiny toddler grinning broadly at his achievements, has only just begun; that of Oliver, considered but not yet conceived, has not yet started, and that of Poppy not even the faintest twinkle in an optimistic parental eye.

Sam goes and sees his father in his bedroom when he visits, as Walter comes downstairs so rarely now. He is desperately short of breath and even if he could get downstairs, it would take ages to get back up again. Walter lies on the left side of the bed and so Sam places himself gently on the other side where his mother, Marieke, has faithfully kept her husband company for the many years of their marriage.

Sam recognises the man in the bed next to him as his father but he is very different to how Sam remembers him. Apart from his pallor, he is quiet, considered and reflective. He does not mention the words death or dying and nor does Sam, perhaps because they are both trying to spare each other's feelings, perhaps because they are frightened to do so, perhaps because they think it unnecessary.

Walter tells Sam he considers him to be a jolly good chap and has no worries about him in the future. He knows that Sam has recently been promoted at work and looks like he is doing well. But his father asks Sam to make sure he looks after his mother. They both know that Marieke is indestructible and will last many more years but she will soon be alone and frightened of the future. Sam promises to do what Walter asks, though the conversation is so general that it is just a matter of quiet reassurance that Walter need not worry about those he is soon to leave behind.

Sam feels a mixture of emotions as he lies there. His gut wrenches at the thought of his father's death and the loss of the man who has been so influential in his life so far.

Further Up the Beach

This is the man who created all those wonderful memorable Bonfire Nights of Sam's childhood, with huge magnificent fires and spectacular fireworks which could be seen for miles across the flat Lincolnshire countryside. The man who bought Sam his first watch and a series of bikes on which he learnt both to balance and to travel at exhilarating speed. The man who risked mortgage repayments in order to give his family of four children their most memorable holidays, first in Scotland where Sam learnt to canoe and later in Denmark where Marieke was born, with its long flat beaches and wild North Sea.

Yet the prospect of his father's death also provides Sam a lurch of hope for the future. He dares to believe that Walter's demise might free him from what has been going round in his head repeatedly and without resolution ever since he can remember and which he knows to be intimately linked with the man who now lies next to him, despite all those powerful positive memories.

As Sam lies alongside his father, he registers surprise, even amazement, that even now, Walter thinks that he has no reason to worry about him because, despite Sam's outward show of being easy-going and positive about everything and everybody, actually he feels crippled inside. Perhaps, like his father, Sam has become a victim of his own success and the mask he wears is the person Walter sees and believes Sam to be.

Sam is flattered that his father is saying all this to him and even wonders whether Walter might know him better than he knows himself. But he is also hurt that his father does not seem to recognise the possibility of the pain he has caused him over the years. Now that he knows his father is dying, it occurs to him that a part of him actually wants it to happen because then he may be able to shed what has beset him since he was a small child and instead look to the future with his own young family. This makes Sam feel very guilty, which is an emotion he already knows a lot about.

When Sam gets home, he spends time at the dining table, working on a piece of writing. This tells the story of his relationship with his father, what he has meant to him and how unhappy and conflicted he has felt since his earliest years but been completely unable to show. It is some years before the first computers, so it is all in Sam's own hand, written and sometimes scrawled with passionate indignation, query and, on occasions, hatred. It is for nobody but Sam but he has read somewhere that writing things down can help people understand and come to terms with them.

Sometimes, Sam feels a sense of release and can almost hear the sibilance of the pressure escaping. But this never lasts and this cheap home-made therapy does not make him feel different or better for long. He keeps his writing in a secret place and shows no-one, not even Chloe, who has heard all about this from Sam and even witnessed Walter in later years. Sam has an idea that one day he will no longer have need of these outpourings but knows that this will never be the case while his father remains alive.

Walter spends his last couple of weeks in hospital, just after Margaret Thatcher has won a third election victory, having already won wars against the Argentinians abroad and the miners at home. Over the last few years, there have been many false dawns to his death but he always bounces back and surprises those around him. Sam visits his father on a hot Sunday afternoon in mid-summer and they talk amicably but superficially. It is now close to the end but there is no urgency or indication that things have once more reached the point of critical.

But two days later, Walter is dead. Sam is certain that he died just before midnight because they get a call at about 10.30 in the evening, telling them to come quickly because Walter is fading fast. He has gone when they arrive shortly after midnight and this new day is the official registered date of his death. But Sam is as sure as he can be that his father breathed his last breath the previous day and the phone call about fading fast is a well-used euphemism, designed to save relatives the worst news until their arrival at hospital.

Now Walter lies in the same hospital bed in which Sam saw him only days before. His is the first dead body Sam has ever seen. His eyes have been closed by the nurses who have also brushed his hair; Sam can tell that this is not his doing because it is combed backwards rather than across. For a moment, he thinks Walter has fooled them again and is just sleeping. But now his face is waxy and his body is without the shallow breath of previous weeks and months.

As Sam kisses his cold forehead, he has an absurd, gut-wrenching fear that his father is now within his power rather than vice versa and that there is nothing he could not do now to settle the scores between them. Sam has no desire other than to say goodbye but he is drawn to the fear of his own power to do wrong because he knows that he will be able to use it to torture himself in coming days, weeks and months.

Sam has been very busy inventing and carefully gathering many such irrational fears around him like storm clouds since he was a small child. By now, he has come to the conclusion that there is something terribly wrong with him but he simply dare not tell anyone who might be able to help him to get to the bottom of it because he is so ashamed.

Sam learns over the following few days that death is a great promoter of adrenaline and false cheer. There is so much planning to do that it feels at times like his family is having a party, rather than mourning the loss of their father. The phone never stops ringing and there is an air of forced, slightly hysterical positivity amongst them.

He and Joy, his twin sister, go the local florist and club together for flowers which will make their brief appearance at the crematorium in a few days' time. They choose a card which says, 'In Loving Memory of Dear Dad'. Sam decides he needs something, a token of permanence, which will help him keep his father's memory alive. So he picks up a spare card with exactly the same sentiment and places it in his wallet where it remains for the next three decades, proof of his enduring love for his father, in case either he or anyone else should dare doubt it.

At the crematorium, they listen to someone who has never met Walter or his family solemnly intoning fragments of his life, and together they heartily sing a couple of hymns. The words mean as little to Sam as the address, but the music and solemnity of the occasion make him well up and he struggles to fight back the tears. Then this brief goodbye must come to an end because another family is waiting patiently in the queue.

Walter's coffin disappears as if by magic behind the chintzy red curtains which open and close by the same supernatural force, and this makes Sam think of Paul Daniels' TV shows which leave everybody in awe of such

Further Up the Beach

trickery. It is difficult to believe not only that his father is actually dead and gone but also that he is physically lying in that expensive shiny coffin. Sam wonders what he looks like now and how much, if at all, he has changed since he said goodbye to him at the hospital a few days ago.

Then everybody disperses and it is back to the family house where there is a good old shindig, and Charles, as eldest son, steps into their father's shoes as head of the family to say a few words to the assembled company. The family is already morphing into something new and different, yet in many ways with the same hierarchy, now with Charles as its head and the younger siblings, Helen, Joy and Sam, expected to fall in line with the new order. Charles has been crowned king, having had no option but to assume the crown, and they are now his reluctant and potentially rebellious subjects.

Finally, it is time for everyone to leave, and when Chloe and Sam arrive back at their own home, it all starts to sink in, albeit in a rather surreal way which makes Sam want to pinch himself. His father is dead and whatever happened between them is now in the past and need never bother him again. Alongside sadness, his loss fills Sam with a sense of elation, the possibility of a new beginning and casting off a lifelong oppressor. It is mid-summer and the warmth and natural light feed his sense of cautious optimism. Despite the season, Sam thinks of fresh untrodden snow and how the future can and must now be different from the past.

He goes into his tiny triangular garden, clutching a box of matches in one hand and his sheaf of writing about his childhood, adolescence and early adulthood in the other. Carefully he scrunches up each individual page over which he has laboured for many hours, kept top secret and shed many a tear. Soon, the incinerator is full and then, slowly and deliberately, Sam strikes a match and watches its contents go up in flames before quickly turning to ash, as his father's body has itself done earlier this very day.

This ceremony, one of Sam's own making and a kind of second funeral in a day, is spectacular, fleeting and final. He cries again, but this time deep sobs, unlike the repressed sniffles of the earlier ceremony. He resolves to continue to love his father, but also to make the next thirty years of his life different from the previous thirty. Dad, he thinks, your time is now over and mine is just beginning.

Before going to bed that night, Sam looks inside his wallet which contains the card saying 'In Loving Memory of Dear Dad'. This reassures him of his love for his father and he vows earnestly that they shall never be parted.

2. GRAND THEFT

Walter and Marieke's bedroom is in the front of their large detached house which houses their family of four young children. This is the only double-fronted house in the long road and has fields at the back and fields at the front. Sam is not sure as a tiny boy what double-fronted means but comes to realise that it means that it has rooms and windows on either side of the front door, making it a house of unusual width in a road otherwise made up of semis. Some of these are extended but none has the natural size and class of Sam's own home where he lives with his mother and father, twin sister Joy, older sister Helen and much older brother Charles.

Walter often tells the story about how Marieke wanted four children but he only wanted three, and how she had managed to get her own way by cannily producing twins. Sam realises that this would have meant that, as the youngest twin, he would not have been born, which is a funny thought he cannot really comprehend. There is Teddy too, their dog, who was Charles's homecoming present after he had been in hospital to have an operation as a small child. Teddy is a great friend to Sam who wishes this black furry mate could talk because he is sure they would have lots to say to each other.

The double-fronted house means that the family's very long garden is absolutely enormous. It is made up of three sections, with a lawn and flower beds nearest the house, then a large patch where Marieke and Walter grow vegetables and finally what Walter calls the sports patch where they can all play games and where there are lots of apple and pear trees as well as blackberries at the end. It is actually four sections long, as there is also a patio which overlooks the rest of the garden and from which Sam has sometimes seen red ants crawling out of the cracks. Loads of them.

Joy and Sam share a birthday but actually she arrived four hours earlier than Sam. She was born at home but Marieke had to be taken to the Royal Infirmary in town to have Sam. This was all in the days before dads were present at their children's births and used to pace up and down in the sitting room, listening to the labour of their loved ones, with a bottle of whisky to help them along.

Sam sometimes goes into his parents' bedroom when he wakes up and asks to be given a 'chest' with his dad. This involves him lying his tiny little body on the upper half of his father's so that his face is just below Walter's and he can see, touch and marvel at the hairs which sprout like magic on his father's chest. Walter knows immediately what Sam means when he implores his father for a chest and he obliges, opening the buttons on his pyjama top and lying flat on his back, finding the time to cuddle and indulge his youngest son in a simple act of flesh on flesh which will make Sam's day.

He wonders whether one day he will also have hairs on his chest like his father but is content to wait and see what

Further Up the Beach

happens. Part of the fun is that Walter lets him reach up and rub his tiny delicate fingers upwards on his face before he shaves for the day so that Sam feels the stiff bristle which awaits the later lathering and wet shave without which his father would never leave the house, together with sports jacket and tie and well-pressed flannels.

Sam does not ever lie on his mother's chest as he does Walter's and dimly realises that she is unlikely to have a hairy chest too. He realises that he must have sucked her breast when he was younger but has no memories of this experience which, like all else, he shared with Joy, whose needs would have been just as great as his own.

When he is older, he wonders how his mother managed this. Did she have one of them sucking each breast simultaneously or did she have a routine that involved one at a time? If she did the first, did each breast have the same amount of milk in it and was this enough to satisfy their respective needs – was there a better breast? Or if she did the second, how did she choose who went first – did she make sure they did this in turns or did she pick up whoever was squawking loudest and let the other one wait?

Walter is 'tickled pink' to be able to please Sam so easily by giving him a chest and Sam feels a deep contentment that there seems to be no competition for this treat. Perhaps Helen, four years older than Joy and Sam, is still in bed, and so too is Charles who probably is no longer interested in such childish games.

In the bedroom, apart from their bed which seems vast to Sam, Walter and Marieke each have their own chest of drawers where Sam supposes, but does not know, they keep their clothes. His mother and father are always either in pyjamas or fully clothed and he has no idea what they would look like without them, apart of course from Walter's hairy chest. On top of his father's chest of drawers, there is lots of loose change which Sam notices in awe because he simply cannot understand how anyone can have such a large amount of money, even though he knows the family is not rich, despite living in the only double-fronted house in the road and having a brand new shiny car in the drive.

Other people think the family is wealthy because of the new car in the drive and also because Sam's father is very 'posh'. He does not speak with a Midlands accent like the locals do and often says how he hates the way people in the village speak, not being able to say 'up' and 'past' like the Queen, whom he loves, and in the way he believes everyone should do. Walter was born and brought up in London and Marieke is Danish, and Sam works out quite quickly that they think they are rather better than the people who live in their road and the village beyond.

Sam wonders whether this is true and whether this means that he is somehow better too. The family's shiny new car is not actually because they are rich but because Walter works as a sales representative and needs to be able to drive for work and impress his customers.

Sometimes Walter lets Sam sit on his lap and drive the car, even though of course he is pressing the pedals and making sure the steering wheel stays under control. Once they were stopped by an off-duty detective, but he and Walter ended up smiling together. Sam notices that his father can be very charming and works out that this can obviously come in very handy in a tight spot.

Sam and his brother and sisters are also allowed into their parents' bedroom on their birthdays while the presents are given and Walter and Marieke drink a cup of tea. They both smoke but do not allow themselves their first cigarette until after breakfast, when they light up and suck in the smoke as if their lives depend on it. Walter is great at blowing smoke rings into the air, and Sam watches with fascination as his father's perfectly-formed circles of different shapes and sizes emerge and then slowly dissipate as they drift towards the ceiling.

Later, on Sam's eighth birthday, he gets a watch and so does Joy. Charles and Helen already had one each on their eighth birthdays because Walter and Marieke always want to be fair with them all. On another birthday, Sam becomes the proud owner of a Morse code set which allows him to beep out Morse code signals to anyone who wants to listen or watch the bulb flash on and off in case he becomes stranded and too far away to be heard. His father made the set himself; it is mounted on a piece of hardboard with red plastic vinyl. On the day of Sam's birthday, it does not work at first and Walter gets very upset because he has worked so hard on it and does not want Sam to be disappointed.

Sam knows that his father has been 'in the war' and, although he is not sure what that means, he is pretty certain that whatever he did was important and brave and somehow involved the use of Morse code. He knows too that Walter was a pilot and got shot down over Germany where he and his crew parachuted to safety. So although there is much that Sam cannot understand, he knows that his father is obviously a very brave man who might have died but did not. Sam is thrilled to receive the Morse code set because it has been made especially for him by his father who is a hero and it also seems a very exciting thing to be able to do. Sam wonders whether perhaps one day it will save his own life, as it must have done other people's in the war.

No-one goes into Walter and Marieke's bedroom when they are not there, so when as a young boy Sam decides he has to do so on his own, it feels very strange. He knows that he has to go in to accomplish something very important and also that doing this is a risky business in case he gets caught. He has to put some change on his father's chest of drawers because he is certain in his head that he has done a truly dreadful thing – he has stolen some of that loose change from his father.

Sam fears he must have done this whilst being allowed in the bedroom after having been given a chest and perhaps his father's back was turned. Worse still, reasons Sam, perhaps he has done this awful thing on the occasion of his birthday when Walter has spent his hard-earned money on his youngest son and given Sam presents he could not really afford. Sam does not know how he can have done this, yet he has a sinking feeling deep in the pit of his stomach that he has done so.

Yet in another way, Sam also knows that he has definitely not done this terrible deed, that something in his head is making this up for reasons that simply do not make sense. He knows he is innocent, yet he is compelled to believe that he is guilty and must make amends because if his father discovers that he has done what Sam fears he might have done, something truly terrible might happen. Perhaps Walter will not give him any more chests. Perhaps he will not give him any more presents for his birthdays to come. Perhaps he will not love him any longer.

There is another possibility in Sam's mind, which is that he has not taken any money from his father but that putting some of his own pocket money (which of course his father has given him in the first place) will be a way of making sure that his father continues to love him in the future as he seems to love him now. A kind of insurance policy, maybe.

So Sam creeps into the bedroom when he knows Walter is out, Marieke is busy and his brother and sisters are playing in the garden. The bed is made, with its 'counterpane', as his father calls it, spread to perfection and there is a pile of loose change on Walter's chest of drawers. The room is extremely tidy, with everything perfectly in place just as his father tells his family it had to be when he was in the RAF and there was a kit inspection.

Sam wonders what else he might find inside the drawers or behind the cupboard doors but he concentrates on the task in hand. He reaches deep inside the pocket in his shorts and, amongst the odd conker and marble, finds several pennies and a shilling piece which he places carefully alongside the coins already there. It is very important that his father does not realise what Sam has been up to, as otherwise he might suspect that the tiny chap to whom he gives chests and presents so willingly has been a thief and in this way betrayed his trust. So Sam mixes all the coins up, opening and closing his eyes tightly several times to check and double check that he has done what he set out to do. Then he leaves the room as quietly as he entered it a few moments earlier.

From the kitchen below, Sam can hear his mother calling for help in shelling peas from the vegetable patch for the dinner they will eat together when his father returns home from work. When, like now, it is summer, they always shell peas sitting on the step of the house overlooking the patio where Sam has seen those red ants crawling out of the cracks they have made their home.

He has to decide which way to go downstairs, either the way they are supposed to or instead, by missing out the first few steps by clambering over the banisters and jumping to make a soft landing on the big step as they change direction. He decides to do the latter and wonders whether this is what it felt like for his father as he made the landing with his parachute in the war. He dashes at top speed down the rest of the wide staircase into the imposing hall which forms the centrepiece of their double-fronted house.

He hopes against hope that what he has just done upstairs will be enough to take away that deep and gnawing feeling of guilt from the pit of his stomach. Just before Sam goes to find the others, he fixes a smile on his face to make sure he looks happy so that nobody will guess what is going on inside his head. Only he knows anything about the vital, secret deed he has just completed in his parents' bedroom, and it is very important that it stays that way.

3. RED ANTS AND ALL THAT

Ants, so far as Sam knows, are black and so the thousands of tiny bright red creatures that swarm in, out and around the cracks of his family patio are unlike anything he has ever seen. A friend of Sam's, Ben, told Sam about how his tortoise was eaten by red ants that entered his shell as he slept unsuspectingly through the winter. When the time came to wake him up, the shell was empty and Ben no longer had a pet, just the husk in which he had previously been housed. Sam did not believe him at the time, but now it is different. He believes every word of Ben's tale, as red ants are there, swarming before his very eyes. They have found their way into the garden of Sam's home and he is scared, very scared.

Sam has a tortoise too. He is called Tommy. He is to make up for the fact that Charles has Teddy (even though Teddy is really a family dog) and his sisters have their hamsters that race round in their wheel all day without ever getting tired. Sam wants to love Tommy the way he loves Teddy, who seems to be able to speak to him and always be his friend. But Sam does not really like Tommy's ugly wrinkly face, nor does he understand why sometimes he chooses to pop it out of his shell to take a look around, whilst at others he shows no signs of life. Sometimes, when Tommy is being inquisitive, he shows Sam how long his neck really is, as he cranes it to see more of the world, making it look as though it is made of wrinkly elastic.

Tommy is not around for most of the winter because he hibernates and Sam finds it hard to be friends with someone who disappears for such long periods. Sam would like to say that he misses Tommy when he goes for his long winter sleep in his little blue house with its red roof. But the truth is he does not, nor does he feel any great wave of affection when spring arrives and it is time for him to wake up and join the living world again. Sam has not really forgiven Tommy for pissing on him when a family photo with all the pets was taken. Sam is certain that poor Tommy could not help it but the thick smelly warm treacle that dribbled on his young bare legs filled him with horror and embarrassment, even though it was not him who had produced it.

Sam watches the hordes of red ants move in silent unison on the patio and feels the terror they create in him. He wishes that Ben had not told him the story about what the same creatures did to his tortoise, or that he had not listened. They seem to have no purpose in mind other than to threaten Sam, his family and his very existence. They have the power to destroy all that Sam has and knows, although he does not understand exactly how that might happen. He tries to reason with himself that this is not going to happen, that the ants are small and insignificant, but he cannot see them as anything other than a naked threat. Sam fears that perhaps one will enter his shoe as he walks across their home on the patio and then others will follow and they will overpower him, maybe when he is asleep. Perhaps one day, unwatched and emboldened, they will clamber up the step from the patio onto the outside porch where Sam sits on the step, shelling peas. Then up another larger step and through the French doors and into the sitting room which goes from the front to the back of the house.

Once this happens, this must surely be the end of Sam and his family because there are so many more of them than there are of his family and they move with such silent determination and in such great numbers that they will be able to achieve anything they want. If they can bring the life of Ben's tortoise to an end, then Sam fears that not only must Tommy be at risk, but so too must Sam's whole family, devoured whilst they sleep by a danger unknown to anyone but Sam, and for which he therefore carries a terrible responsibility.

Sam tells Charles about them but not about the terror he feels deep inside. He hears Charles tell their mother but does not want to tell her himself in case she thinks he is making a fuss about nothing. Sam hears her say to Charles that perhaps the red ants will put them all out of their misery! Sam's mother is funny like that, joking about serious things, such as being miserable. Sam hopes she does not really mean what she says about being 'in misery' and is sure that she does not. She does not seem to be miserable to Sam, although she and his father are very busy with four children to look after so they must both be very tired at times, which might occasionally make them miserable. Marieke does not seem to be in the least bit worried about the red ants and Sam says no more about them because he fears that it will only make him look even more stupid than he has already made himself look.

Sam is happy shelling peas because they are not like the tins of dried peas he and his friends can buy and put in their pea-shooters. Like red ants, dried peas have started to worry Sam too, because another friend told him about how a friend of his got one stuck up his nose and that once there, the moisture made it germinate and swell. Sam starts to take extra care when he is using his pea-shooter in case he should absent-mindedly or accidentally put one up his nose and the same thing happen to him, which might mean that his life would be in danger because of the rapidly-swelling pea.

Of course, Sam knows that in order for a dried pea to end up in his nose, he would have to actually make an effort to put it there. But however much he tries to remind himself of this, he fears that it could happen accidentally in a careless moment when his defences are down and he is not thinking carefully or watching himself as he must. He imagines morbidly the pea taking over first his nostril, then his whole nose and eventually working its way towards and into his brain, so that he is gradually destroyed.

When Sam blows his nose on the clean big white handkerchiefs his mother produces on Mondays, her washing days, he always checks again and again in case an enlarged and hairy pea emerges amongst the snot but this has never happened. This means that either Sam has not put one there or it has yet to come out. He knows in his heart that it is the first of these but still fears that it is the second and that it is only a matter of time until his demise at the hands of a monster hairy pea. Sam recalls telling someone at home that he is worried about this but there is too much

Further Up the Beach

else going on to fret about silly things like this and the conversation is quickly lost.

The picture of a hairy swollen pea up his nose makes Sam fear threats from other things which also look scary. Now he is in the orchard at the bottom of the garden, picking up windfalls from the apple trees for his mother to make the apple crumble she makes every week for pudding after their roast dinner. Joy and Helen are helping and together they try to fill the old battered tin bucket they have been given. They work together and Sam is on his own, with stuff buzzing around in his head.

He looks up at the old gnarled apple tree and sees the familiar bark, leaves and apples. Then he spots something easily as scary as the red ants and the idea of a dried pea up his nose. In fact, Sam finds it scarier than both of them combined. The bark and branches of the tree are in places sprouting mould which is white, moist, furry and misshapen. It is not part of the apple tree and yet in other ways it is. It is an alien which has attached itself to an innocent bystander.

Sam instantly recognises this as a new and vital threat, which brings terror to the core of his being because he knows it must also have the power to attach itself to him and destroy him, as might be the fate of the apple tree. He decides he must make sure he does not touch it or even go anywhere near it. He washes his hands again and again when he goes inside even though he has not touched it, just to make as sure as he possibly can that its malevolence is kept firmly at bay.

Sam plucks up his courage and shows his sisters the mould on the tree, which he describes as 'woolyafus'. There is no word like this in the dictionary but it describes to Sam what he is seeing with his own eyes. He tells his sisters it is scary and hopes they will take him seriously. But for now, they are knitted together in female fraternity and Helen has the eyes and ears of his twin, Joy, the other part of Sam. They descend into giggles of hilarity at Sam's pathetic discomfort, yelling 'woolyafus' again and again and making him feel silly for telling them anything was the matter. Sam realises how stupid all this must seem to them and wishes that it did not terrify him in the way it does.

Sam resolves not to mention to anyone else anything which, to him, represents pathetic but devastating fears, as his attempts to do so have not been very successful so far. Instead, he chooses to lock them inside himself and simply pretend that all is well, remembering always to smile a lot to help prevent anyone spotting that anything might be wrong.

He has heard his father describe his youngest son as a 'jolly easy-going chap,' unlike Charles, who is a right handful and hates being thwarted or losing at anything, perhaps because, as the eldest, he has had so little experience of this. Sam quickly identifies 'easy-going Sam' as his escape route, the disguise he must wear and continue to perfect.

He worries briefly that he might let things slip by saying things under his breath which might give his true thoughts away, so he devises another plan to get over this. This plan involves whistling when anyone else might be around. This means that he will not give away any of his innermost thoughts and also that he will confirm himself as the kind of chap Walter tells everyone he is and perhaps wishes him to be. Walter whistles a lot too, and so, in Sam's young mind, this all seems to fit together quite nicely.

He decides that he will also wash his hands again and again, sometimes right up to his elbows, to make sure that he does not have anything on them which might harm either him or his family, were he to accidentally touch them with unwashed hands.

This all seems to work quite well for now, though it does not stop Sam encountering more and more of these obstacles as he goes about his business in the garden at home. Marieke is using weedkiller in the garden and Sam spots warnings all over it about how it is harmful if swallowed and how it must be treated with very great care. He makes himself steer clear of it, but despite the fact that he has not even touched it, he worries about what it might mean if he had done so. It might transmit itself from his fingers to any object he touches, and in that way, to someone else in his family who would be poisoned as a result. Or worse still, Sam might use the weedkiller to deliberately harm members of his family, even though he desperately does not want that to happen.

The only way of making sure this does not happen is for Sam not only to avoid touching it but also to wash his hands even more regularly, just in case he has accidentally done so. Thank goodness for soap and water! Sam devises an ever-more elaborate system for washing his hands in a way that it will surely be impossible for any germs to do him or anyone else any harm. Not only does he soak and wash them up to his elbows, he also washes each individual finger many times to make absolutely sure it is without trace of anything which might have the power to harm anyone.

When Sam is a little older, he is cycling to his piano teacher's and spots a dead bird on the roadside. In his mind, this instantly contains a package of deadly germs which might infect him or his piano teacher who has promised to help Sam pass his first piano exam. Sam dare not stop to look, but the notion takes root immediately in his head that he has touched the bird's corpse and has himself become dangerous and infected as a result. He arrives for the lesson in a wild panic and lets out a garbled explanation about how he has seen a dead bird on the way and how he needs to wash his hands. His piano teacher looks puzzled but lets Sam do so before he settles down to play her his piece and show how hard he has been practising.

As he begins, he starts to doubt that he has locked his bike outside her house. Walter works so hard to make sure Sam and his brother and sisters all have bikes which are safe and roadworthy and he does not want to have to tell his father that his has been stolen. Also, he loves and needs his bike to get him round the village.

When Sam emerges an hour later, the bike is still there, as of course it must be, since, despite the anguish caused by the dead bird, Sam did not forget to check time and time again that he had locked it. Just to be completely certain.

4. D DAY

Sam knows that school is a place you start to go to when you reach a certain age because Charles and Helen have been going for as long as he can remember. His older brother and sister get up in the morning and disappear for the day, leaving Sam and Joy together with Marieke, whilst Walter is at work to earn money to provide for his family. Sam knows nothing about school other than that he must go and that Joy will go with him, and that once they have arrived at this unknown place, they will start to learn things like spelling and sums. They will be taken and fetched from school and it will not be until they are older that they will have to find their own way there. It is only a walk away, right in the centre of the village, although there is also a bus which stops just outside, by the church.

Sam expects that the other children will speak the way his father hates so much and is always telling them they must not. Sam wonders whether he will be able to work out one language for home and another for the playground, as he has already heard that some of the local kids have called their family 'posh', which does not sound very friendly to his young ears.

When Sam and Joy arrive on foot, they go into separate playgrounds, Sam into the boys' and Joy into the girls'. He feels a panic rising in his chest straight away, as they are only very rarely separated and Sam does not like it when this happens. Joy, on the other hand, strides towards her own entrance as though she has been doing it all her life, but not before reassuring her twin brother that things will be fine.

There is a great big black wall facing Sam as he enters the boys' playground, which is teeming with little boys like him running around and shouting, as well as some older ones who look like they know their way around. One boy called Patrick, who has a big smile and jet black hair, has a football and invites Sam to take it in turns kicking it against the black wall, which he does. Sam likes playing football and thinks that he might be quite good at it one day and perhaps even become rich and famous. Others join in and they all morph into pretending to be the favourite footballers they have glimpsed on the television or been told about by their dads or older brothers.

Suddenly a large lady appears from round the corner and claps her hands together, bringing the whole playground to order immediately. Silence falls as if by magic as she places her finger on her lips, glaring at anyone who does not take the hint. The boys are instructed to run once round the playground, then to get their breath back by touching their toes. Then they are each given a small bottle of milk to start them off for the long school day ahead. Sam's milk tastes warm and not nearly as nice as he has on his Weetabix or cornflakes every day. But he decides that if football and

Further Up the Beach

drinking milk are what school is all about, it cannot be all bad, although by now he is starting to wonder and worry again about when he will be reunited with Joy.

From here, the line of little boys is directed in single file and hushed silence to the main hall for assembly where, to Sam's relief, he spots Joy again. She is with a girl called Judy and he remains with Patrick, who he ardently hopes will remain his friend because of his big smile and the fact that he has a football. There are climbing frames on the wall of the hall, from which Sam works out that things other than assemblies happen here.

The headmistress, Miss Dartington, tells the serried ranks of tiny faces where to look in their hymn books so that together they can sing the right songs. Another teacher, whose face cannot be seen by Sam, hammers out a hymn on the piano and this helps them all sing the right tune, just like the older children who have done this hundreds of times before. When they have finished singing, Miss Dartington begins something called the Lord's Prayer. This is about someone called 'our father', but Sam twigs that it is not about an actual father like his own, but a kind of father figure who everybody thinks is great and has lived in the past.

Unlike the hymn which has gone before, the words are not written down and the next generation of God's tiny unsuspecting souls are expected somehow to know them. Sam does not, but adopts the tactic of sometimes running slightly behind the others and following in their wake, and at other times pretending to say something but really saying nothing at all. Once, he catches a teacher's eye and fears that she knows what he is up to, so for a while Sam just looks

David Monk

down and focuses hard on his feet from which he hopes he might gain inspiration. His shoes are very shiny, as his father says they must be polished every day for school, even though, as Sam looks along the row, few, if any, others seem to have had this treatment.

Whatever the exact words of the Lord's Prayer, it comes to a decisive end with the word 'Amen', at which point things relax a bit and there is quite a lot of chatter. Then a teacher tells Sam to help move the forms back into place. He looks completely blank and thinks the teacher has told him to help to move the fawns. Whether they are talking about forms or fawns does not actually make any difference because Sam does not know what either is. Eventually, he decides they are saying 'forms' and that these must be the benches they have all been sitting on which must be moved to the edges of the hall so that PE lessons can take place.

Sam wonders why it is that everyone apart from him knows that a little school bench is called a form. Perhaps 'form' is something just common people who live in Lincolnshire say and is part of the language people there speak, which his father often describes with real feeling as 'ghastly'. But this is Sam's home; he has to live here and understand what is going on. He worries about how many other words there might be which he does not know and everyone else does.

They spend the rest of the morning with their new teacher who will teach them everything for the whole school year and then they will be old enough to go into the next year. She is called Miss Morrow and, unlike Miss Dartington, has a kind face which reminds Sam of his mother's. But despite (or perhaps because of) this, Sam suddenly starts to feel like

Further Up the Beach

he wants to be at home with Marieke and begins to cry. Not just little sniffles, but great big uncontrollable convulsive sobs. Joy tries to comfort him and so does Miss Morrow, but he is inconsolable, bereft and cut adrift from the place he wants to be, at home with just his mother and Joy who never leaves his side and feels part of him, except when they are at school and Sam cannot have her all to himself.

A little later, a large bell sounds and Sam hopes and prays this is the signal to go home but it is only lunchtime. Some people say it is dinner time in the middle of the day, but Sam's father says that that is only because they do not know any better because they live in Lincolnshire rather than the south of England, and in fact the meal eaten in the middle of the day should always be called lunch.

The hungry discombobulated children sit down at long tables, four down each side and one at the head. The boy who glowers down at Sam and the others from the end of the table is an older boy called Ricky who is wearing a badge, telling the others that he is the table monitor. His job is to serve out the food and encourage everyone to eat what is in front of them. Sam has learnt to always scrape his plate clean at home because, although he and his family never go hungry, he is aware that it costs a lot of money to buy food for their large family.

Marieke and Walter talk sometimes about how people were very hungry in the war and how lucky everyone is now to have enough food to fill their bellies. All Sam knows about the war is that both Walter and Marieke were 'in it' and that when his father was a prisoner of war, he also became the 'ration king'. But they look very old to Sam and so he reckons that was all a very long time ago, perhaps in another century, or at least what Marieke calls the 'olden days'.

One new boy asks Ricky for a large portion and Ricky growls back at him,

'You'll get what you get.'

Sam supposes that this big scowling boy at the head of the table is a kind of modern-day ration king and wonders whether his father met with these kinds of hopeful requests in the same way when he was in the war. The boy hoping for extra gets a little less than he otherwise might have done and it crosses Sam's mind that table monitor Ricky is probably rather a bully who is best avoided. Sam wonders whether the new boy who asked for more is hungry because he lives on the council estate where he has heard on good authority that the poor people live and some even have fleas, as well as speaking with a Lincolnshire accent.

Across the table, Sam notices a tiny boy with round glasses held together with sellotape. He is called Danny and Sam noticed him when they were playing football earlier. He has had his lunch served out and is now looking at the big pile of gristly meat and mound of cabbage with alarm. He takes a mouthful and chews and chews until eventually it goes down. He looks around the table at the progress others are making, then tries another mouthful which eventually he swallows. Then his eyes fill with tears and he dares to say he can eat no more because he does not like it.

Sam immediately feels sorry for him because he has himself only just stopped crying, so knows what it is like. Also, Danny does not have a twin sister like Sam has to look after and protect him. Everyone else clears their plates and soon there is just little Danny with a pile of uneaten food

Further Up the Beach

left on his plate and the fearsome Miss Dartington glaring at him from her dais.

Then she is out of her chair in a flash, dragging Danny out of his seat and to the front. His muffled sobs become hysterical screams as she parades this squirming bundle of terror in front of the whole school, telling of his wickedness in not eating food which has been put in front of him when there are so many hungry people in the world. She drags him back to his chair and stands over him whilst he tries to put another forkful of the cold congealed mess into his mouth.

But either he cannot or will not. So out to the front he goes again, dragged by Miss Dartington who by now is purple with rage. As she raises her hand with Danny cowering below, Sam notices she has a large mole on her nose. She smacks Danny repeatedly and tells him again and again that this is what happens to little boys who are so ungrateful as to not eat the food that is prepared for them. Sam sees the panic in Danny's eyes. There is no escape for him and he wails even more loudly than Sam did before. The rest of the school looks on, mesmerised and terrorised in equal measure by Miss Dartington's fury at Danny's shocking ingratitude. Sam's plate is clean and he is reassured that, whatever happens after lunch and before home time, at least he will not be beaten in front of the rest of the school, as has been Danny's fate.

What happens after lunch is a blur for Sam, other than he soon begins crying again because he does not want to be at school and also because he cannot help thinking of deathly pale little Danny with the sellotaped glasses. Sam longs to be as strong and confident as Joy, who comforts him and tells him that it will soon be time to go home. But it does not seem to be, and even when home time does arrive, Sam knows that from now on, he will have to come to school every day for the rest of his life. His only consolation is that Joy will be with him and she will be able to help him cope.

Sam has never been separated from her from the moment they were born and before that, they nestled together like two peas in a pod in Marieke's tummy. At home, they are often called 'the twins', rather than Sam and Joy, and all the photos they have of them at home and on holidays are ones in which they appear together, often in matching outfits that Marieke has knitted or made with her old Singer sewing machine. They sleep in separate bedrooms, Joy with Helen and Sam with Charles, but apart from that, they are rarely apart.

When finally they are able to go home, Sam has stopped crying but his eyes are red from all that has gone before. He catches a glimpse of Patrick, who smiles that big reassuring smile and says that he will see Sam again tomorrow and he will bring his football again. Sam tries to smile back and look brave but struggles to do so.

Then he looks for Danny who, after his lunchtime humiliation, is nowhere to be seen amongst the children and parents who throng outside the school playground. Sam wonders how Danny will summon up the courage to come to school again and how he will cope without a twin sister to help him. He wonders too if Danny will tell his mother and father what happened at school and whose side they will be on.

But tomorrow is another day to be dreaded and in the meantime, Sam clings tightly to Joy's hand and, with her leading the way, they make their way together to where

Further Up the Beach

Marieke is standing to take them home. They return home on the bus which costs a penny halfpenny each, which Sam decides is great because he is feeling very tired from all his exertions.

On the bus, Sam spots a man he has seen once or twice before. From the front, he looks like anyone else, but from behind, it can be seen that he has a heavily-veined boil the size of a football on the back of his head. Sam tries not to stare but cannot resist. It is both repulsive and compelling. He wonders how this man must be feeling about that and thanks his lucky stars that at least he does not have to worry about such a thing. Perhaps, he thinks, cheering slightly as the bus stops outside their home, there is nothing for him to worry about after all.

5. FURTHER UP THE BEACH

All mealtimes are very similar in Sam's house, though there are some when Walter is not there, as he is still at work. But when he is at home, he and Marieke sit at either end of the big dining table which is extended to its full length by pulling out the leaves at both ends. Sometimes, this doubles up as a table tennis table and the family has great fun playing table tennis. At mealtimes, Sam and Joy ('the twins') sit next to each other on one side and Charles and Helen on the other.

The table has been laid by Sam's sisters who are expected to help Marieke as things in the kitchen reach a crescendo, and Sam and Charles are expected to help Walter with the clearing up when it is all over. This includes wiping the new shiny smooth formica tops which Walter has recently spent many hours fitting in their kitchen.

Walter always washes the dishes, first by rinsing, which he calls 'stacking,' then washing with soap and water, then by rinsing again one final time with piping hot water. Charles and Sam stand armed with checked drying-up cloths and they dry up, as crockery and cutlery come steaming off the highly efficient production line.

The dining room has a big bay with 1930s leaded windows which look out from the front of the house, and from Sam's place at the dining table, he can see the big fir tree in their front garden. The kitchen sits on the same side of the house and looks out over the huge back garden. Plates of food are sometimes carried between the kitchen and dining room and there is also a trolley which Walter has made in his garage which helps with moving all the crockery and cutlery from room to room.

This is before Walter has the bright idea of building a hatch between the two, a job he starts on impulse after lunch one day. He jokes that perhaps the house will fall down but it does not, and as he breaks through to the other side and gradually makes the opening bigger, the family has fun poking their heads of various shapes and sizes through the new hole, marvelling at the miraculous new connection between what before seemed to be completely separate universes. When it is finished, it makes everything much easier, although it does not change what actually happens when the family is all sitting down and the food is on the table.

All this takes place on just one side of the double-fronted house, which is all that all the other semis have, unlike Sam's family, whose sitting room is on the other side of the hall, stretching all the way from front to back.

Sam understands very quickly that two things are very important to his father. The first of these is fairness. There is plenty of food on the table, but it has not always been like this for Walter and Marieke, and Walter has an

Further Up the Beach

overwhelming desire to ensure that food is equally divided between his hungry growing children. When it comes to second helpings, he and Marieke will usually do without and share what is left between the children.

This always fills Sam with astonishment and he marvels at how one human being can do this for another. He decides that Walter wanting him to have a full belly, perhaps fuller than his own, shows that he loves him. Walter is even kind when sometimes Sam is greedy and takes more food than he should, putting this down to his youngest son's over-enthusiasm and the size of his eyes compared with the size of his belly, rather than castigating him for his greed.

Walter does not tell his children much about the actual war, other than his having been a prisoner of war in Poland and appointed 'ration king' by other men in the camp. Sam realises that this must have been a very important job, as all the men must have been very hungry and needed to trust completely that the person serving out the food would do so without fear or favour.

Sam also knows that Walter ended up in the camp because he was a bomber pilot in the RAF and was shot down during a mission over enemy territory. He parachuted from his burning aeroplane to safety and spent the remainder of the war in captivity. Sam listens to how Walter and Marieke met after the war in a hospital where Marieke was a nurse and Walter needed to have plastic surgery on his face after the aeroplane he was flying crashed and he had to have some of the flesh from his hip (which Sam never saw) grafted on to his nose, which was reconstructed.

Walter has a medal for bravery too for going to get help for an injured crew member and walking many miles to do so. So Sam is quite certain that his father is not only a hero but also one who must make sure that every morsel of food is shared out equally between the hungry mouths that gather round the family table, of which Walter is the head. That is why he is so determined to make sure his children get equal shares of other things too, like all getting watches on their eighth birthdays and all having bikes to ride around the village as they get older.

But there is something else which is also very important to Walter, even more important than making sure his family all have full bellies. It is what he calls 'polish'. Polish is what Sam must have in order to make the grade in life. It is about the way he speaks, ensuring that he does so as Walter speaks, without a hint of the 'appalling' Lincolnshire accent that surrounds the family in the town which Walter derides and often calls a 'one-horse' town.

To do this, he tells Sam again and again that he must copy him and not the friends who surround Sam every day, so that his future life will not be blighted by the affliction of a regional accent, as theirs will certainly be. Walter sometimes laughs at the ugly way people around them speak, but at other times it makes him very angry because he feels that it is just him standing out against all this regional ugliness.

To protect his family, Walter creates a kind of South East fortress enclave in the heart of hostile, one-horse Lincolnshire. This means that friends only rarely cross the threshold of the family home and that the two worlds of Sam's family and friends only mix when it is absolutely necessary to do so. Others who live around Sam and his family, who do not demonstrate Walter's painfully-acquired polish from his earlier RAF experiences, are sometimes described by his parents as 'peasants'. Sam is unsure of the meaning of this but quickly conjures an image of a country yokel who wears a crooked, tatty hat and chews ruminatively on a piece of straw, though he can see no-one in the village meeting this description.

Walter and Marieke, of course, are struggling to understand the highly complex and unforgiving social strata of their time and how they can best help themselves and their family negotiate its many perils.

When his father becomes angry about all this, Sam feels worried and scared. It seems to him that Walter hates the local accent so much because he fears what it might do to Sam and his brother and sisters if they were somehow to become infected by it.

Walter always makes sure that the family tunes in to the Queen's message to the nation on Christmas Day and Walter tells them proudly that she speaks with a perfect accent. Sam realises how much his father loves and cherishes the Queen, which is something Sam cannot feel, however hard he tries. Walter tells Sam that he would dearly love to send him to elocution lessons but cannot afford to do so, which makes it even more important that Sam listens very carefully to all that his father has to tell him.

But polish is about more than just the way Sam must speak. It is also about manners at the table, which means that mealtimes are at the very centre of understanding how all this works. Walter explains how not only must Sam never place his elbows on the table, but he must also always tip his soup away from him, rather than towards him, as this is what those who know no better will do. When Sam leaves the table, he must always say, 'Excuse me'. He must never ever go the toilet during a meal but instead always make sure he does so beforehand. On the table at teatimes is a little knife to be used for the butter and spoons for the jam to prevent them becoming infected with bread or toast crumbs, and Sam is frequently reminded that these must be used at all times.

There are also very important rules away from the dining table, which include learning how to shake hands properly, always standing when a woman enters the room and never forgetting to walk on the outside of the pavement when walking with a woman so that Sam can take any splashes. Sam also learns through multiple repetitions the importance of how he should be dressed. Walter never leaves the house, even at weekends, without a sports jacket and tie and warns Sam of the utmost importance of never failing to carry a handkerchief, as to fail to do so would be as bad as going out without his underpants.

Walter says that little boys who are sent away to public school are taught all of this until it becomes part of them, a kind of 'veneer' which shines and sparkles in any company and marks them out for who they are. He regrets bitterly and sometimes angrily that he cannot afford to send Sam and his other children to public school but instead is determined to do his best to make sure that they can imitate those who do.

At family mealtimes, Walter holds the attention of his family, including that of Marieke, and seems to know no way of conversing other than with himself at the centre of the conversation. Usually, there is no conversation as such, other than the topic chosen by Walter. Sometimes, he can be very amusing and people always talk about his great sense of humour, but at others, he is focused solely on his

Further Up the Beach

instructions and exhortations about speech and manners which will define Sam in the future.

This is a lot for Sam to take in and think about and it gets even trickier when Walter reinforces his points about all this with warnings about what will happen if Sam does not successfully absorb all he is being told.

If this were to happen, Sam learns that the parts of him beneath the veneer, which is so much thinner for Sam than for those who are lucky enough to be sent to public school, will be exposed for all to see. In Walter's words, Sam will be 'branded – absolutely branded, old boy'. Walter looks very serious when he says this and Sam realises that he desperately does not wish his youngest son to have to endure this pain.

The idea of being 'branded' is very frightening to Sam and he worries that he is almost certain to get things wrong at some point in the future, however hard he tries not to. Although Sam understands that this may not include the physical pain of someone pressing a red hot iron on his skin, it is clear that it will involve public embarrassment and humiliation of the highest order.

Walter talks a lot about how he sees his job as throwing Sam and his brother and sisters 'further up the beach' than he himself was thrown. Sam thinks this means that he wants to throw him to a safe place where the sea will not engulf him but he worries that if he is not strong enough or has not listened carefully enough, he might end up like perhaps his father was and become swallowed by the fast-approaching tide, out of control and at risk of eventually drowning.

Someone with a window on the past would have known that Walter's own father, who served and was decorated in the Boer War, as well as fighting in both the First and Second World Wars, spent time in a London workhouse when he was a young child. To Walter, cossetted as a child by his mother and much older sisters, his father quickly became a remote and elderly figure with whom he enjoyed little closeness or companionship.

Later, Walter himself had some very narrow scrapes with the kind of branding he talks about so often with Sam, having left a state school without qualifications and entirely bereft of polish as he has come to conceive it.

As a very young man in the loud and crowded mess of his squadron of Bomber Command, Walter quickly became aware that there were two classes of people. The first spoke suavely, without a trace of Walter's Cockney accent. They possessed confidence, poise and panache. They laughed together at things Walter did not understand and exchanged glances with each other that could only be shared by other members of the same club. They called each other 'old chap' or 'old boy', which Walter had never heard before and which made it hard to remember their names. They sometimes ate separately from the rest and at other times everybody ate together. When Walter ate with them, he became self-conscious in a way that he had not experienced previously in his short and sheltered life, surrounded by his parents and adoring older sisters. He had always been a bit clumsy with his knife and fork and did not always even bother with both of them if just a fork would do.

But here Walter noticed that the people with the poise and panache always used both and worked the knife and the fork as if they were one, effortlessly guiding slippery, challenging combinations of different food from plate to implement and into their mouths. Walter had been taught as a child not to speak with his mouth full but saw now that somehow this other class of people managed to do so without everybody being able to see what they were eating or spraying the contents of their mouths over others. He could not work out how this was possible.

One of them laughed at Walter over dinner and asked him who taught him to eat like that. Before he could reply, his interrogator smirked to his chums and they began a private conversation about something Walter was not supposed to hear but appeared to be about how their former public schools were deadly rivals at cricket and rugby. On another occasion, one of the 'chaps' pointed out a bit of dried snot on the end on Walter's nose and sniggered as Walter struggled to find and dispose of it with his finger, finally offering him his own pristine handkerchief so long as Walter promised to return it in the same condition.

Poor, sensitive Walter missed his mum, dad and sisters and wondered why they had not told him about this alien and hostile world. He burned with embarrassment and shame and decided that he would now have his work cut out if he wanted both to fly an aeroplane and to hold his own in this new, unfamiliar and rarefied company.

He watched and learnt quickly the tricks of the trade at the table and made good progress with his knife and fork. He tried calling other people 'old chap' or 'old boy' and was comforted that they did not hoot with laughter when he did so. He knocked the roughest edges off his Cockney accent, adding h's and t's where previously there had been none. He sent home for a supply of handkerchiefs and shed a tear when his mother responded quickly to his request, as well as enclosing a note saying how much she and Pa were missing him.

With all these speedily-acquired additions, Walter became practised at being something he was not, but desperately wanted and needed to become. He worked hard to develop an outer veneer of confidence, bonhomie and charm which those officers in the mess displayed so effortlessly.

His own, of course, took more effort because it was not really him. It did not belong in him in the same way as it did in those other chaps because theirs had been grown from a tiny seedling, whereas his own had been hastily and inexpertly grafted on. As a result, he could only truly feel master of himself and his destiny by becoming the centre of attention and behaving in ways that made up for an inner insecurity which knew no depths and threatened to reveal him as a snotty-nosed oik who was just pretending to be one of the chaps.

Learning to fly was difficult but no more difficult than Walter's own self-reinvention. It also required him to be massively brave, as his sweaty hands took control of the Lancaster for the first time with responsibility for its crew and the bombs stacked into its huge distended belly. Mates whom he felt he had known all his life because of the intensity of the experience did not always return from 'ops', and he and the chaps developed a dark sense of humour to cope with these cruel and unpredictable events.

Walter became an officer during his time as a prisoner of war, as well as a hero amongst his mates, following a brief escape from the camp during which he and fellow escapees initiated acts of sabotage against the enemy, including

Further Up the Beach

electrical installations and on the railways. But despite this, he never felt quite like those chaps he remembered from those early days when he so painfully became a man in a cruel and class-ridden world.

The memories of death and destruction, coupled with his own personal exposure and humiliation at the dinner table in the mess, would never leave Walter. Nor would the adrenaline that coursed through his young body as he fought to lift the Lancaster off the ground and later bring it to a safe landing. By the time he returned home in 1945, he felt he knew enough of the tricks of the trade to get by in whatever his post-war life had to offer.

As peace settled over Europe, Walter's attention turned to marrying Marieke and raising his family in the world for which he had fought so hard and risked his life many times over. What no-one knew is that his terrifying wartime experiences had created in his psyche a severe form of post-traumatic stress. However, this condition was little-known or recognised at the time and it was expected that returning heroes would simply get on with their lives as if nothing unusual had happened. This would leave Walter's nerves jangling and on edge for the rest of his life, and in future years would disturb his equilibrium, as well as those around him, at the most unpredictable times. Walter had successfully escaped from his burning aeroplane and was now a free man but he remained imprisoned by his wartime traumas and would never forget the cruel lessons of the officers' mess.

But little Sam does not have that window on the past as he sits as a young boy at the table, feeling hot, sweaty and worried about whether his next move will be the right one.

He hears his father talking about what a happy family they are and assumes that he must be right. In many ways, Sam thinks perhaps he is, as he is certainly happy some of the time.

Like when Marieke discovers that someone has been pilfering raw jelly from the larder because just a few messy squares remain of the block that she knows she bought. Walter makes everyone laugh by laughing at Sam's thieving of the jelly and advising that it is always best to steal a whole block, as this would raise fewer suspicions. Then there is more hilarity as Walter tells a story about how he took Teddy for a walk down to the end of the road and allowed him to do his business outside the house of a furious neighbour who threatened, Walter thinks quite unreasonably, to post the turd back through Walter's letter box. Sam feels sorry for the neighbour, but on the other hand, reasons that hers is only a semi and therefore perhaps his own family's detached house gives them the right to allow Teddy to perform there.

Sam often hears his father say what a contrast their happy family is to Uncle Andrew's. Uncle Andrew rules his children with a rod of iron and is said to even have a stick at home to keep his sons in line. Walter says he would never hit his children because he does not believe in corporal punishment.

But Sam is still scared and worried about what will happen if, despite all Walter's best efforts, the 'veneer' he develops is just not thick enough and the real Sam pokes out. Then surely he will be branded, humiliated and alone on the beach, gasping for air and quickly swallowed by the merciless sea. Probably, fears Sam, much worse than being beaten by the stick he is almost certain his father does not possess.

6. BATH TIME

The family bathroom is very much like any bathroom in the early 1960s, with a great big white enamel bath and matching sink. There is no toilet in it, as that is next door on its own, and nobody has ever heard of showers. Both look out over the garden at the back of the house.

When Sam opens the window in the bathroom, he can see the outhouse which is stuck on to one part of the back of the house. This houses three rooms, one with shelves on which sit the family's old boots and shoes which Walter requires to be arranged with not so much as a shoe out of place, another an old toilet and the other contains the coal for the coal fire heating they have in the downstairs sitting room. They do not have any heating upstairs, apart from tiny electric fires which the children are only allowed to put on briefly if there is ice on the inside of the windows, which is not unusual.

The outhouse has a flat roof and sometimes, when Sam is looking for excitement, he climbs out of the bathroom window and drops lightly onto the flat roof below before continuing his descent by shinning down the drainpipe between the flat roof and the ground. Nobody else knows about this, as it is Sam's secret and only his.

Although he plans to keep it this way, he feels strangely confident that, if by any chance he were caught in the act, his father might understand. Sam thinks that what he is doing might remind Walter of his brave wartime exploits, and in particular, escaping from a prisoner-of-war camp when nobody was watching. Perhaps Walter might even admire Sam for his daring escapade. Perhaps, deep down, Sam even hopes that his father might discover him doing this so that he might witness his son's bravery.

But tonight will offer no such excitement. It is a winter's night, the windows are all shut tight and it is bath time. When Sam gets older, Charles and he will have a bath on Wednesdays and Sundays, and Joy and Helen on Tuesdays and Saturdays. When they were younger, Sam and Joy used to bath together but now they are too big to fit into the same bath. So now they are kind of in between times which means that, to save water, Sam is to hop into his twin sister's bath as soon as she is finished.

He does not mind when it is his turn to go second, as he loves the feeling of entering a tepid bath, before then feeling the rush of heat as Marieke tops it up with piping hot water. Sam takes care not to place his small feet under the hot running water but loves getting as close as he possibly can to the source of the intense heat without actually burning himself. It is like when he fills his hot-water bottle with boiling water from the kettle and slowly can bear to put his tiny feet on that intense heat. Much as Sam loves his twin sister, he also adores having Marieke all to himself for a little

Further Up the Beach

while, as he stretches the full length of the bath and wonders if he will ever grow too long for it.

Joy has been in there a while with Marieke, and Sam hears his mother calling to him that it is his turn to take the plunge, as Joy has nearly finished. He undresses to his pants and goes to have a pee (known as a tinkle) in the next-door toilet, from which he can hear Marieke and Joy having fun together. Rather than pulling up his pants and entering the bathroom covered up as he normally does, Sam decides to join their fun by rushing in to the bathroom, making as loud a noise as he knows how to announce his grand entrance.

The other feature of Sam's grand entrance is his tiny little bare penis which flaps up and down and from side to side in a comical way as he runs, jumps up and down or twists his little body round. It seems to be part of him, yet not something he can control as he can other parts of his body, such as his arms and legs. Sam is sure that the combination of this perky little fellow, along with his rendition of *Z Cars*, his favourite TV tune, can only increase the fun Marieke and Joy are having together.

But Sam is wrong, terribly wrong. He is more wrong than he has ever been in his entire life so far. He pushes open the door which Walter has just panelled with hardboard and peers in through the steam. Both Marieke and Joy look up, his sister from the bath and his mother from the stool with a cork seat that Walter has made because he is very good at woodwork and loves wood as much as he says he hates metal. At this point, Sam loses track of what Joy might be thinking because Marieke's reaction is so overwhelmingly powerful.

She does not laugh as Sam was sure she would, or choose to grab and tickle his tiny wriggly body before dumping him in the bath and telling him to get himself washed, as that hot stream of water gushes from the tap. Instead, Marieke's face is frozen at the sight that greets her, first with disbelief, then horror, before finally coming alive with intense fury. She yells at the top of her voice that Sam is a disgusting little boy who should know better. She orders him back to his bedroom at once and tells him to go straight to bed. Sam will not be allowed downstairs again that evening for a story, nor will he have his normal bedtime drink of hot milk and sugar.

Sam runs from the bathroom in floods of tears, knowing now that he has done something truly terrible but unable to understand what has provoked this most severe of reactions from the woman who is his mother and whom he loves very much. Sam gets into his pyjamas and goes to bed, where he covers himself with blankets and hides from the world, burning with embarrassment and shame and wondering what he can ever do to earn his mother's love again. He hears Marieke and Joy talk in hushed tones about his misdemeanour as they leave the bathroom and thinks that perhaps Marieke is explaining to Joy exactly why what he has done is as terrible as it is.

Sam hopes and prays that Marieke will come to see him in bed, where he continues to whimper, but he hears them both go downstairs to join the rest of the family. He cannot hear what is going on downstairs but he knows everyone else will hear about what has happened and why he is not being allowed downstairs, which makes his pain even harder to bear.

Sam thinks of Teddy who is his friend and who sometimes gets what Marieke and Walter call 'over-excited', which means that an enormous pink sausage-like object appears as if from nowhere hanging from his underbelly and almost touches the floor. Sam has never worked out exactly what this is but now wonders whether, when this happens, Teddy has done something as bad as he himself has just done. Teddy has shown a part of himself which is private and got into big trouble for it.

When this happens, Teddy is ushered out into the garden until his excitement has worn off. But nobody explains to Sam what has actually occurred, why Teddy is in disgrace or what that pink dangling monster actually is. Sam wonders where it suddenly comes from and why. Sam is excited when he receives presents for his birthday or Christmas but that does not happen to him.

Now Sam is exiled to his bedroom, just as Teddy is sometimes to the garden, and Sam wonders whether his four-legged friend feels as unhappy when this happens as he does now. Sam longs to see and cuddle Teddy and wishes they could talk about all this because he knows Teddy would understand and might be able to help him. But Teddy is downstairs with the rest of the family and Sam will have to wait until tomorrow until he sees him again.

One thing now crystallises in Sam's mind, however, and that is that what he has done and who he has been in his earlier exuberance is somehow a problem. It made Marieke more upset and angry than he has ever seen her. Perhaps she is now in the 'misery' she talked about when she heard through Charles about Sam's fears about the red ants on the patio. He may also have done the same to Joy, to whom he looks to protect him from things he is scared of.

Sam wonders how his naked little body can have caused so many problems and decides that perhaps it contains powers and secrets that he simply does not know about.

He wonders whether he will be able to gradually earn back his mother's love and trust by being more like his twin sister, who does not seem to get into these sorts of scrapes. Perhaps he might do this by helping to pick apples, pears or blackberries from the end of the garden or by shelling peas or broad beans from the vegetable patch for dinner.

Sam resolves to listen out for all such opportunities. He will watch Marieke carefully as she works feverishly on her grand old Singer sewing machine, making dresses for his sisters, or sits with her knitting needles, one anchored under each arm, knitting jumpers for one or other of her children. Sam hopes desperately that one day his own misery will be at an end and that his dear mother's face will show forgiveness for the sin he committed in the bathroom earlier this evening.

Sam knows the rudiments of his mother's life before him, just as he knows a little of his father's. He knows that she was the daughter of Aksel, a Danish sculptor, famous within that small country, though not outside of it. An unhappy relationship with her stepmother led to Marieke leaving home early, at loggerheads with Gerda, the much younger woman who had supplanted her mother, and angry with her father from whom she became largely estranged. Later, Marieke trained as a nurse and worked in a TB sanatorium in Denmark when war broke out in 1939, witnessing the occupation of her country until 1945.

Once war was over, this brave, independent woman spread her wings and became a nurse in England, where she met and married Walter before giving birth quickly to Charles, then Helen and finally Joy and Sam. Word that her mother's death, in an age before Sam was born and cannot begin to comprehend, was the result of suicide reached little

Further Up the Beach

Sam via the hushed tones of his sisters who, together with Marieke, form a tightly-knit female trio he longs to be part of in the absence of anything similarly intimate with Walter and Charles. But it is only a direct question from Sam to his mother towards the end of her long life which leads her, amidst continuing pain and shame more than seven decades later, to admit that her mother committed suicide.

But this is never spoken about. Nor is anything of what the window on Marieke's life reveals when pushed ajar inadvertently by Sam many years later, including the fact that in the 1920s, Aksel made an application to the Copenhagen Court for Kristina, his wife and Sam's grandmother, to be detained in an institution for the insane.

Kristina's incarceration in a secure psychiatric hospital lasted nearly three years, during which time there was no contact between her and Aksel, nor between Kristina and Marieke. Kristina blamed herself for the separation from her daughter, at times appearing resigned to this, whilst at others desperate to be reunited with her.

After many false hopes of discharge which she craved but frequently felt herself unworthy, Kristina finally took advantage of being allowed day release as a seamstress and chose not to return to hospital but to escape instead. She was last seen wearing a new hat as she hurried purposefully through the back streets close to the hospital which had become her home and prison. Only Kristina knew where she was living during those last months of her life, during which time police were alerted, with a view to returning her to secure conditions.

She chose to end her life by swallowing pills she had bought from the local chemist, after she had decided to leave no note and had carefully drawn the curtains of the upstairs room of her shared accommodation. Kristina was found by an old man living at the same address, her body already cold and stiff and with only a few possessions to her name, including three treasured hats, two notes of 100 kroner and the change from the pills she had bought to end her life earlier that day.

However wide open this window on the past is pushed, no-one can know whether Kristina was truly unwell and Aksel had no alternative but to remove her from the family home to a place 100 miles away when Marieke was not quite seven years old.

An earlier photograph shows both parents and the tiny Marieke at around the age of two. They are all looking very smart, wearing hats and done up as if the weather is very cold. Here, Marieke is being held by Aksel, with Kristina empty-handed, other than for her handbag held in her right hand. Is Kristina perhaps at this point not being trusted to hold her daughter? Or is Aksel's firm grip on Marieke completely insignificant, explained simply because he had both hands free to handle their precious offspring?

It is not known whether Aksel turned to Gerda in his desperation over the plight of his wife, and their relationship developed from there. Nor is it known whether his relationship with the much younger woman was a factor, perhaps the critical factor, which triggered Kristina's emotional ill-health, placing her conveniently out of sight whilst alive, and permanently so after her decision to end her own life.

Regardless, in the mind of Sam's mother, Aksel became, simply and squarely, the reason for the loss of her beloved mother, at first temporarily through hospitalisation and later permanently through the taking of her own life. For Marieke, who had to make sense of all this as she grew up, it was her father Aksel's philandering that sparked the catastrophic loss of her own mother, which remains an unhealed wound until her own dying day.

Seeing the world through this telescope, Sam's misdemeanour in the bathroom on that cold winter night becomes a tiny cog in a much bigger wheel, comprising past shame, loss and untrammelled emotional pain. In Marieke's mind, the negative power and havoc that male sexuality is capable of wreaking knows no bounds. She had little or no opportunity as a child or adult to consider alternative perspectives, and she, like Walter following his earlier traumas, is expected simply to get on with life and look to the future as if nothing remarkable had happened.

When all these unresolved emotions are unexpectedly triggered in the bathroom by her youngest son, who means no harm and is just looking for love and fun, she finds it impossible, despite the depth of her love for Sam, to find in her heart forgiveness or redemption for him.

Despite the coldness of the season, a tiny yet potent seed of shame from the mother plant is caught in the chilly winter breeze. It rises momentarily and then is buffeted by the wind before settling and then germinating in Sam's fertile mind. Here, it joins the shoots of a rampant and ugly weed, already growing out of control as a result of Sam's unsuccessful attempts to make sense of all that he must do to please his loving but frightening father. For this apparently carefree little boy, who always makes sure to have a smile on his face, life now becomes even more complicated.

7. GARAGE TALK

At the side of the family's big double-fronted house, there is a wooden garage where Walter spends a lot of time making things. He loves wood from which he can create furniture out of nothing. Smaller pieces of wood are placed in his old metal vice to hold them steady so that they can be sawn, planed and drilled.

Sam holds larger pieces for Walter, such as the hardboard he uses to panel the old-fashioned internal doors so that they are no longer old-fashioned dust traps. Sam marvels as he watches his father sawing down a perfectly straight line, as the dust and shavings from his saw gather gradually above. When they start to obscure his line, but not a second before, Walter blows them away in one big blow and they float to the ground as he continues to the end. At this point, Sam has to hold extra tight, as he is taking the weight of the almost-separated piece of wood and knows that a second's carelessness on his part will mean that it will rip and the neat edge will be ruined.

Sometimes, Walter lets Sam hold the saw and tells him patiently to use its length and not press too hard but let the saw do the work instead. Sam learns to blow the sawdust away like his father does. Slowly, Sam gets better at following his way down the line Walter has carefully drawn in bold pencil, but the young apprentice doubts that he will ever be as good as Walter at this.

Walter is in his garage doing woodwork and Sam is kicking a football on his own on the top lawn next to the patio. When Walter calls Sam to the garage, Sam thinks it is to hold a piece of wood for him. But instead, he takes unsuspecting Sam completely by surprise by asking in a super-casual voice whether he knows how babies are born. Sam has not given this much thought to date but does not think he does, so Walter takes this as his cue to reveal the mysteries of life.

In a nutshell, he tells Sam that the man passes a seed to the woman to make a baby, but that this (a baby) does not always happen and when it does not, a woman will not need to feed the baby and the result will be that she will not be able to go swimming. When this is the case, Sam must on no account ask why she is not swimming on that particular day. This seems to be about all there is to it.

There are no new words in what Sam has heard Walter say and in some ways, Sam thinks it all sounds very simple. But in every other way, it is very puzzling because these bits of information do not seem to add up to anything he can begin to understand. He wonders what this seed looks like, how big it is and how exactly this transaction takes place. For some reason, his father's words conjure up an image in Sam's head of something round and very large being handed from the man to the woman, both of whom struggle under its considerable weight.

What exactly occurs from that point and how that is linked to babies being born or women not being able to go swimming is also not at all clear. Sam goes swimming every Sunday morning with his family, so reasons that perhaps one of his sisters or his mother will not be able to go at some stage in the future. He wonders, if he were to ask a woman why she was not able to swim that day, whether this might result in him being 'branded', like everything else he needs to remember would do, like how he speaks and behaves, particularly at the dinner table. So Sam makes a note to try to remember this but secretly hopes that this awkward situation will never arise.

During the time that Walter is imparting these jewels of wisdom, he is concentrating intently on a piece of woodwork, which means that his eyes do not meet Sam's during the conversation. Then, quite abruptly, Walter asks if Sam has any questions. Sam can see his father's eyes glancing towards the door, from which he gets the feeling that he would like Sam to exit sooner rather than later.

Sam's understanding of what Walter has tried to tell him is so slight that he cannot even formulate any questions for Walter which would make sense. He has neither understood a single word Walter has said to him, nor begun to comprehend why his father has chosen this moment to talk to him about this. So Sam says what is simplest and what he is pretty sure will please his father: that he does not have any questions. Walter nods and resumes his woodworking, while Sam returns to find the football and carry on practising kick-ups on the lawn.

Sam senses that Walter is very pleased indeed, perhaps even extremely relieved, to have got this particular conversation over with. Sam promptly forgets all about the conversation with Walter and assumes that Joy will at some point be able to help him understand what he needs to when the time comes. After all, there is no point in trying to make sense of all this just now.

8. UP HIGH (1)

Each Saturday morning, Sam goes with Walter to the baker's a few miles from their home. Today, it is just Sam and his father because his sisters are doing something with Marieke, and Charles is doing his own thing. Walter dresses at his most casual in sports jacket and tie and Sam climbs into the passenger seat of the car alongside him.

How his father can drive and control this big chunk of metal is completely beyond young Sam, as is his father's ability to find his way around, even when they are driving on roads he has never driven on before, like when they go on holiday. To Sam, both seem to be near-impossible feats and just add to his belief that his father is truly invincible. Today though, they know where they are heading. Sam is going to have a haircut and Walter will leave him at the barber's while he goes to pick up the bread for lunchtime.

Walter sometimes has fun driving towards a main road where he has to stop, but jams on his brakes at the last second so that drivers on the main road think he is going to crash into them. He does this today and laughs at the alarmed expression on the face of a driver on the main road who does not know that this is just what Walter calls a 'jolly jape'. Sam wonders what this might feel like to the person driving the other car but he laughs too because he is with his father and that is all that matters. Together they will come to no harm and Sam knows that the other people won't either, although they might not realise it.

Walter and Sam are in a brand-new purple Zephyr 6, which is another reason for them to feel powerful because most of the cars on the road are much older and slower than theirs. The house whose drive they have just left and the car they are now in together suggest that they are rich, even though Sam sometimes hears Marieke and Walter talk in worried tones about being very short of money. Sam has even heard his sisters talk in hushed whispers about how their father has missed payments on the mortgage and used the money to take the family on holiday to Scotland instead.

There is an empty chair at the barber's which Sam clambers into when invited to do so by a ruddy-faced man with a large and friendly smile. Walter explains that he will be back shortly and the barber asks him how Sam's hair is to be cut in the meantime. Walter says simply, 'Short back and sides,' which is how Sam's hair has always been cut for as long as he can remember. Walter's is the same and he says that this was how all the 'chaps' in the RAF had their hair cut and this is how it must be done. Sam saw The Beatles on TV the other night who have much longer hair, but Walter is unwavering in his dislike of this and considers that short back and sides must continue to be the order of the day instead.

Sam does not really know what to talk about with the barber once Walter has gone, and for a while, they just size each other up as the barber snips expertly at Sam's curly hair. Marieke used to call him 'curly top' when he was younger and recalls fondly how, before Sam could talk properly, he used to reply indignantly, 'Me no turl top!' Sam looks tiny in the mirror as he sits cowering below the barber's clicking scissors which remind him of the click clack of Marieke's knitting needles as she knits furiously in front of their little black and white TV in the evenings.

Then suddenly Sam is being asked a question by the smiling barber who pauses to hear his response. The question is, how would Sam like his hair at the back? Sam thinks of The Beatles and the new song everyone is singing called 'She Loves You' and wonders what it might be like to look a little bit like one of them, even though his hair is not only curly but also fair, quite unlike that of the lads from Liverpool. But he wonders about his father's instruction that this should, like all previous haircuts, be 'short back and sides' and what Walter might think if Sam were to end up looking different to what he is supposed to. The barber wants to get on with it, get Sam out of the chair and start on his next customer, so he asks the question a bit differently, providing tongue-tied Sam with more help as to how he might respond.

This time, he asks whether Sam would like him to leave it a bit longer at the back, as that is what everybody else is wanting to do nowadays. This makes Sam realise that this is exactly what he does want and so he replies that that would be great. He starts to feel excited about coming out and looking a bit different to how he has in the past. He hopes that his father will not notice, or if he does, that he will not mind.

A few minutes later, the barber holds a mirror up behind Sam's head and asks if this looks okay. He has only left it a tiny bit longer than normal and has not run the clippers up the back of Sam's head as he normally does. Sam says he is happy with it, though he registers disappointment that he still does not look the slightest bit like the lads from Liverpool. The rest of the time passes quickly, with just a quick conversation about football.

Before Sam knows it, Walter has returned, clutching the still-warm bread from the baker's. He pays the barber and together he and Sam make their way back to the car. Walter comments on what a ghastly regional accent the barber has and takes the opportunity to remind Sam why he must never speak like that. Sam nods his ready assent, breathing a sigh of relief that Walter did not inspect the barber's work before they left and concluding that Walter has either not noticed or, if he has, has chosen to say nothing.

But Sam is wrong, because after lunch that day, Walter notices when he sees Sam from behind. His father wants to know how it has happened that Sam's hair is short at the sides but not at the back where the clippers have not done their normal work. Sam's heart misses a beat and he explains what passed between the barber and him and that this is what he chose.

Walter does not rant and rave or blow his top as he sometimes does but instead, very quietly, tells Sam that they must return to the shop that very afternoon to have the job completed. Sam tries to tell his father that it is his hair and this is how he wants it, but these words somehow evaporate

Further Up the Beach

in the space between them. Walter looks very serious, his jaw set firm with an iron determination, and Sam knows that he will only lose if he chooses to argue. Although Walter usually does not hit Sam like he says Uncle Andrew does his boys, Sam is actually scared of his father and knows that he will not rest until his youngest son's hair has been restored to the regulation requirement.

An hour later, Sam is back in the same barber's chair, with Walter being as nice as pie with the barber and asking him to cut more off at the back. Then the clippers are being run up the back of Sam's head, leaving him with that crisp feeling which he used to enjoy when he was younger, and he ran his finger over where it had just been cut. Sam no longer looks even the tiniest bit like any of The Beatles.

More importantly, he feels angry and upset in a way he cannot possibly explain. Not only has he not been allowed to have his own way with regard to his hair, which belongs to him and him alone, but he has also been made to look small and stupid by being taken back to the barber's to have it put right. Sam would like to tell Walter why he feels angry and upset but knows that the only thing that matters to his father is that Sam now once again looks as Walter feels he should. Sam feels something deep in the pit of his stomach which makes him want to scream, shout and sob out loud but he knows this will not be allowed and that Walter's steely determination will instead become anger, which makes him feel petrified.

This feeling stays with Sam and he does not know what he can do to make things feel better and to try to communicate with his father about how he has made him feel. Walter is now cheerful and whistling as they drive back together, content that order has been restored and his authority remains undimmed. Sam, though, feels as if he has been placed in a vice like the one Walter has in his garage for woodwork, squeezed so tight that Sam cannot and dare not move, and under his father's total control.

Sam is still feeling bruised as the new week begins. Walter fixed Sam's beloved bike over the rest of the weekend and also reminded Sam once more over Sunday lunch as to how he must speak and behave in order to avoid being 'branded'. Although Sam knows that his missing hair cannot be magically regrown, he also knows that Walter can see nothing wrong with what he did at the barber's. Sam fears that he is destined to continue to have short back and sides for as long as he can imagine into the future. He also realises that Walter will always tell him what to do, dominate him and brook no dissent.

Father and son see each other at breakfast before Walter leaves for work but Sam does not want to say goodbye as he normally does before his father drives away. He also does not want his father to know where he is so that Walter can say goodbye to him and assume that everything is alright and that Sam feels happy. Because, for Sam, everything is not alright at all and he actually feels deeply unhappy.

So, before Walter goes to work, Sam quickly and expertly climbs the big fir tree in the family's front garden, which he has climbed before but has not told anyone about, not even Joy. From here, he can see but not be seen, hear but not be heard, and can think and feel what he wants.

He sees and hears Walter getting ready to get into the car below, looking at his watch, as he is worrying that he will be late for work. He asks Marieke urgently where Sam is so that he can say goodbye, as he already has done to the rest of the family. Walter is looking and sounding frantic with worry and cannot understand where Sam can suddenly have disappeared to. Walter does not say it but Sam wonders whether he is worrying about the possibility that Sam may have run away since eating his breakfast or even been kidnapped. He calls Sam urgently again and again but Sam stays silently in his den, quiet as a church mouse and enjoying his aerial view and even perhaps Walter's distress. Finally, Walter drives away for the day, leaving Sam watching the disappearing car from the treetop and feeling that at last he has perhaps succeeded in communicating something of the strength of his feelings to his adamantine father.

Later, when the coast is clear, Sam slinks down the tree and makes up some cock and bull story to Marieke about where he has been and what he has been up to. By this time, Marieke is busy with household chores and so Sam seems to have successfully avoided any interrogation which might have led him to have to give the game away.

When Walter comes home, he seeks Sam out and tells him how worried he was that morning because Sam was nowhere to be found. Sam thinks Walter must have spoken to Marieke during the day and heard that Sam was safe after all. Walter does not ask Sam where he was hiding and Sam does not tell him. Although Walter must know that something must have made Sam behave like this, he does not ask him about it because, as far as he is concerned, rules are rules and he has ruled, as he must, on the length of Sam's hair. Perhaps he does not even register that Sam's behaviour is linked to what happened at the weekend in the barber's chair.

But he does tell Sam that he is his father and so he cares about him. Sam nods, listening but not understanding how, if that is so, his father can behave in the way he has. Perhaps Walter understands that Sam is not convinced. Still Walter does not enquire what was and is the matter and still Sam does not tell him because he knows he will only be crushed again, as he felt over the weekend. Then Walter concludes the conversation by saying something very important,

'Always remember I love you, old chap.'

Sam treasures these words over the coming years, just as he treasures the occasions in the future when his father rescues him when he is afraid and in need of help. But the mystery of how Walter can truly love him and at the same time behave as he sometimes does remains unresolved in Sam's troubled mind. He cannot decide which is the more baffling, this or the still puzzling question of how babies are born, what this seed is all about and how exactly it gets passed from the man to the woman.

9. I PROMISE TO DO MY BEST

Most children of Sam's age go to Cubs or Guides and Sam is no exception. He looks smart in his uniform, some parts of which are hand-me-downs from Charles. He particularly likes his neckerchief and toggle which are brand new. Sam walks to Cubs from his home up to the village hall about a mile away and then home again. Although he has to be away from Joy for the evening, which is very unusual, he does not mind too much. They play lots of games at Cubs and run around a lot. The young Cubs also get the chance to do proficiency badges for different things which then get sewn onto their dark green jumpers. Sam plans to take lots of these and knows that Marieke will be able to sew them on for him, as she is a fantastic sewer and knitter.

There is a thin dark-haired woman in charge called Akela who is a bit like the teachers at school but more relaxed. Everybody is in little groups called Sixes, each of which has six boys, of whom one is the Sixer and another the Second. They all have to do what Akela says and the Sixers and Seconds are like Akela's eyes and ears in the groups, as, although she seems very good at spotting things and even claims to have eyes in the back of her head, she cannot keep them all under control on her own. Sam wonders whether one day he might become a Second, a Sixer or even an Akela, if boys can become Akelas.

He learns to say the Cubs' promise at the beginning and end of the evening about doing his best, doing his duty to God and to the Queen and helping other people. Sam's is not a religious family, although they always tick CofE on any form which needs completing and go to church every month or so, as Marieke and Walter believe that it is their duty to educate their children about the ways of God, if not believe in Him. So, although Sam now knows the Lord's Prayer by heart because he has to say it every day at school, he does not really understand what religion is all about, nor what it means when some of his friends tell him they have been 'confirmed'. Sam does not think he has been confirmed himself but is not sure why not or what this is exactly.

But Sam does understand the bits about doing his best and helping other people and he thinks that Walter will like the idea that he is promising to do things for the Queen because his father loves and respects her so much. Sam wonders whether his Cub pack is a little bit like being in the Army or the Air Force, and when Akela orders them to stand to attention with their feet close together before allowing them to relax 'at ease', with feet slightly parted, he thinks of his father and the stories he has told about the parade ground.

Sam learns to salute too, with two fingers held together above the brow. This makes him feel both funny and proud

Further Up the Beach

at the same time. He cannot decide whether he likes or hates doing this, as he is not actually sure what it all means or what exactly it is for. Sam thinks that one day Walter would like Sam to follow in his footsteps and go into one of the forces as he did when he was a young man. But Sam does not want to have to fight in a war like his father did, and anyway, he is unsure what people in the forces have to do if there is no war on.

One night, Sam is walking to Cubs and has just set off down the road when he sees a group of older boys in front of him. They are not heading to Cubs but are walking slowly and not having to hurry as Sam is, as his prized watch is telling him that he has to get a move on or he will be late, which Akela does not like. Sam recognises one of the boys ahead as Charles's friend Billy, who everyone says has a glass eye, as it never seems to blink like the other one. There are also several older lads strung untidily across the width of pavement, meaning that Sam will either have to stay behind them and move at their pace and be late or summon up the courage to overtake them.

It is a dark evening because the clocks have just gone back and this makes Sam more scared than he would have been had it still been light. The older boys do not know Sam is behind them or how he is feeling, but with every step he takes, he is feeling more and more scared and trapped by the difficult choice that confronts him. If he tries to overtake them, they will almost certainly recognise him as the kid from the posh house and hurl abuse at him. Or worse still, they might chase him and threaten to beat him up. Sam doubts whether his Cub uniform will be much protection and wonders if that might even make it all worse.

Sam panics and decides to do neither but instead runs back home to safety, where he finds Walter finishing the washing up. He blurts out a story about the big boys ahead of him on the pavement not letting him pass. Deep down, he hopes that that will be that and he can now spend the rest of the evening at home, without having to go out on a dark night and promise to do his best to Akela. But that is not going to happen, because before he knows it, Walter has stormed out of the house and Sam is being ordered to follow.

Walter quickly catches up with the gaggle of lads and starts bawling at them, demanding to know what they mean by not letting Sam pass. They look surprised, shocked even, at the strength of Walter's indignation and try to tell him they did not even know Sam was there. There is a brief debate, during which Sam insists that they knew but had not let him pass and they are therefore not telling the truth.

The older boys part under Walter's watchful gaze and Sam dashes past them, just making it to Cubs before Akela blows her whistle to start the evening. Sam does not know who his father believes and wonders whether Walter's fury is with them or himself for being such a coward. Sam worries that this exchange might mean that he will be marked in the village on a future occasion, but at least tonight's problem has been sorted and he has been rescued. As he dashes past them, Sam catches Billy's eye and is as sure as he can be that he sees the glass one blinking, just like any normal eye.

10. RESCUE

Walter and Marieke signed the form months ago saying that Sam will go to Cub camp and it all seemed so far into the future to Sam that he has not given it another thought. He is not sure what he thinks about going away camping and wonders what it will be like not to sleep in a house but in a tent and what exactly they will do all day. But the good news for Sam is that it is only for a weekend and is very local, only a few miles away from home.

Although Sam worries about this a bit, his mind is taken off it completely by an event much bigger than him and his family which absolutely everyone is talking about. It is not a serious event like the earlier Cuban Missile Crisis, when the newsreaders on the family's grainy black and white TV looked very serious and Sam heard Walter and Marieke talking anxiously about how they could all die if the Russians did not back off. As far as Sam knows, the enemy must have done so because everyone is still alive and people have stopped talking about the Russians.

David Monk

Now though, it is an event which instead seems to make everyone very happy and excited. It is the 1966 World Cup, and when the sliding concertina doors on the TV are opened and the TV has warmed up, Sam sees a clip of the England manager Alf Ramsey saying that he thinks England can win not just a game or two but the actual Cup itself. Sam thinks Alf's voice sounds a bit like his father's and wonders if Alf's father made sure his son speaks like this so that Alf could be thrown further up the beach in the same way Walter is trying to throw Sam. Sam wonders what Walter might think if Sam were to become a football manager when he grows up.

World Cup fever starts slowly with England's 0-0 draw against Uruguay but hots up over the next few weeks, and before long, England have beaten Argentina and Portugal to make it to the final against West Germany. Everyone, including Sam, loves Eusebio and is sad when he and his team have to go home. But they all hate Argentina because they are very bad sports, and Sam sees headlines calling them animals, with one of their players even refusing to leave the pitch when he is sent off.

The scene is set for the final which will kick off at 3pm the following Saturday and everyone begins to wonder whether Alf Ramsey might be right and England will soon become champions of the world. Sam is very excited too until he realises with horror that he will be away camping from Friday night until Sunday and so will miss the most exciting event of his whole life so far. He knows very little about camping because the family always stays in farmhouses when they go on holiday, but he is as certain as he can be that there will be no TV at camp.

Further Up the Beach

Sam has no option but to go because he cannot think of an excuse not to. They arrive on Friday evening and he spends his first night under canvas, surrounded by excited Cubs who want to stay up the whole night chatting. Before they go to bed, Sam meets a man in uniform called Pilot who is in charge of the group. Pilot is drinking a cup of tea from a metal mug and smiles and says that tea always tastes better at camp.

Once in bed, Sam thinks about how Walter always says he must have a good sleep to recharge his batteries and comes upstairs to smack his bottom if he is still reading when he takes Teddy for his last pee and perhaps a crap outside the stroppy neighbour's house. Sam knows this will not happen tonight but he wonders how he might feel without his batteries recharged.

When silence eventually falls over the camp, he remains awake, thinking about the next day's mighty football match he is going to miss and wondering whether there might still be a way round it. Suddenly, his mind is made up. Sam has a plan which will need him to tell a lie but hopefully this will be worth it, as he will be able to watch the game after all. He starts to imagine feeling sick, really sick, and how he can look as ill as possible when daylight breaks and England are only hours away from the greatest moment in their history.

He wakes feeling as right as rain but finds Pilot to tell him that he has been up half the night being sick in the hedge behind the tent. He is questioned about how he feels now and whether he is starting to feel better. He looks as sad as he possibly can and replies convincingly that if anything, he is feeling slightly worse. Pilot consults with his helpers and a decision is quickly reached that Sam must return home for fear of infecting the rest of the camp. Walter arrives by lunchtime and, before Sam can believe it, he is back home in the bosom of his family and watching the England players warming up before kick-off.

They are not normally allowed to watch much TV but this afternoon is an exception and even Walter, who is not a football fan, seems excited. During a lull in the action, he goes to the top drawer of his desk and produces six bars of Cadbury's chocolate, one for each of the family. He does this a couple of times each week as a treat, although no-one ever knows exactly when he will pull this rabbit from his hat, to the delighted squeals of his beloved brood.

Sometimes he grumbles that it is stale and complains to Cadbury's who send him lots of free bars to say how sorry they are. Once, the family is invited to look round the Cadbury's factory in Birmingham and spends all afternoon there sampling chocolate off the production line which leads to Sam feeling very sick indeed.

Now, as Sam sits quietly on the settee (which Walter says is actually a couch, whatever anyone else might call it), he is asked whether he feels up to eating a bar and replies weakly that he might perhaps nibble gently on a square or two and see whether his stomach is able to take in more food after the ravages of the night before. He eats as gingerly as he can manage, but by the time it is 2-2 at the end of normal time, he has pretty well polished off the whole bar. Walter and Marieke enquire how he is feeling now, but fortunately he is not questioned more closely because people's minds are on other things, as England are now within a hair's breadth of winning the World Cup.

Further Up the Beach

When Geoff Hurst scores his controversial goal in extra time, all worries about Sam's mysterious stomach bug recede, and by the time Hurst scores his final goal to make it 4-2, Sam is miraculously and completely recovered. When Bobby Moore goes to collect the Cup from the Queen, Sam decides that perhaps when he is older, he might look a bit like the England captain, as, like Bobby Moore, Sam has fair wavy hair, although he is still not allowed to grow it. As Sam's resolve to look like the England captain when he is older grows, Walter is gazing admiringly at the Queen and all that she is and represents to him.

Soon afterwards, the TV is switched off again and its concertina doors pulled across the screen. Alf Ramsey was right about England winning the World Cup. Most importantly though, Sam has been rescued from Cub camp by his father. Sam decides that Walter is not only a wartime hero but also a very kind man, so long as Sam does what he is told and never, ever forgets about that polish, which will be so important to him in the future.

11. TWO WHEELS

Sam has had two wheels for as long as he can remember. First he had a scooter and then a bike. None of them was new because bikes are expensive, but in the same way that Walter always makes sure his children all have the same amount of food and are given watches for their eighth birthdays, so too they all have their own bikes to ride around the village on.

The countryside around them is quite flat and great for biking. Apart from cycling regularly to his piano teacher's, Sam is allowed to visit friends in the village centre, about a mile away. Sometimes he heads out to where the houses end suddenly and open country begins and where the washbrook is, which is basically a muddy stream where Sam and his mates muck about and have a good time.

Although he can never get over how it is possible to balance on two wheels, Sam adores his bike and the freedom it represents. When he is riding it, all the worries buzzing round in his head seem to disappear by magic, carried away with the wind as it rushes exhilaratingly against his face and body.

Walter is brilliant at mending bikes and making sure they are kept in good working order. It is very important to him that they, and therefore his precious children, are safe, and he inspects Sam's regularly, often spotting something like a brake cable that needs adjusting or brake blocks that need replacing. Walter has all the tools he needs in his garage where they are all arranged with military precision and he is able to find easily exactly what he needs.

Walter much prefers doing woodwork than mending bikes but never hesitates to pull Sam's bike, or those of his brother and sisters, in for repair when it is needed. Sam knows that when he rides it again, it will be completely safe and he trusts his father with all his heart to do just that. Sam has never seen Walter actually ride a bike but assumes that he used to do so when he was a young boy like Sam.

Sam has fallen off his bike loads of times because he rides fast with no fear and little appreciation of danger. When he takes a tumble, Walter wants to hear how it happened and usually gives Sam advice about how to make sure it does not happen again, so that he stays safe in future.

After a spectacular fall one evening on an unmade road where new houses are being built, Sam returns home, scarred and bloody with multiple cuts and bruises. Walter examines and then mends his mangled bike, and tells Sam that gravel and speed do not go well together. He is right, as Sam's deep cuts and wounded pride testify. Soon though, his bike is back in commission, with Walter having worked some magic, and perhaps also with the help of the local bike shop where he goes for spare parts and to do specialist things.

Now Sam is cycling along the road where his friend Danny lives, who has new glasses now and is apparently

Further Up the Beach

recovered from his beating and humiliation on the first day of school some years ago. Sam takes his eye off the quiet road for a moment and sails at full speed into a parked car. He is badly jolted and sore as he picks himself up off the ground and nervously examines his bike and the car for damage. Both seem basically okay and Sam gets back on, having learnt something else about safe biking.

Fortunately, there is no-one around who has seen the incident and Sam is particularly lucky that the owner of the car is not there, as they might have found some damage to their vehicle which could have been a big problem for him. He feels rather stupid about this and therefore keeps this incident secret at home, managing to keep his bruises hidden until they have faded to nothing.

After a series of second-hand bikes, Sam's twelfth birthday approaches when he is to get a brand new machine. He finds it hard to sleep the night before he and Walter go and choose it because he is so excited and can think of nothing else. They go to the bike shop a few miles out of town, close to the new school he and Joy have just started going to by bus. Sam really fancies a bike with drop handlebars like all his friends have. However, Walter is certain that for everyday use, straight handlebars are best. Sam wonders reluctantly whether perhaps his father may be more right about this than he is about the length of Sam's hair, on which he continues to rule with a rod of iron.

The bike Sam eventually chooses is dark royal blue and has three Sturmey Archer gears on the right-hand side and a shiny new bell on the left. Walter says that gears will help Sam keep his bottom in the seat whilst cycling up hills, rather than standing on the pedals which he thinks is not good for the bike. Its chrome wheels sparkle, free of rust and dirt and fresh from the factory. It is more beautiful than anything Sam has ever seen before or can imagine. He vows to himself to always look after and cherish it in the future. He has in his head a good idea of what it means to Walter to buy his youngest son his first ever new bike and Sam is sure it has cost him a lot of money which he is certain that his father does not really have.

Not only does Sam ride his bike all over the place as he has ridden previous ones, he often does something else to it. He cleans it very carefully with soap and water, meticulously washing first the handlebars and frame, then the mudguards and finally the space between each spoke. Then he dries and carefully polishes it with a dry cloth until it gleams again as it did in the bike showroom the day he first set eyes on it. This cleansing process has nothing to do with ridding himself of things like germs, though he still fears these might harm him, or worse still, his family. It is to do with something else which Sam has not yet worked out.

In the meantime, Walter notices all this going on and responds positively, pointing out the pride Sam is showing in his bike to Uncle Andrew when he visits. Uncle Andrew nods gruffly and asks Walter why Sam is spending so much time doing this. Uncle Andrew does not hide his view that he thinks this all a bit odd. Maybe Walter does too, though he is not letting on if he does.

Meanwhile, Sam just carries on polishing and making his beloved bike gleam brighter and brighter. Nothing will deflect him from doing what he wants and feels he must do.

Perhaps he is thanking Walter over and over again for having bought him the bike. Perhaps he is showing his father how much it means to him and how he can trust Sam to look after his precious possession. Perhaps Sam wants to make his bike shine in a way that he fears he will not be able to, which he knows, because Walter tells him, must lead to him being 'branded'. Perhaps Sam is also asking, even begging, Walter to offer him his love and approval because, although he is sure that he will always be physically safe and well-fed, he fears that deep down, something else is terribly wrong. He cannot find the right words to describe what this might be, but knows that he must do all he can within his puny power to put right that deep sense of dread.

12. A LITTLE SNIP

It is now some years after the conversation in the garage. Sam is having a pee and gets a pain as he is doing so. He notices blood mixing with his pee and calls his father to see. Walter inspects Sam's early adolescent willy and is very kind about it, telling Sam not to worry but that they should go and see the doctor to make sure that all is well.

Soon afterwards, they are heading up to Dr Heinemann's surgery in the village. Dr Heinemann is an ancient old man, even older than Sam's parents. He smokes a pipe, stinks of tobacco and speaks through his nose, so that it is difficult to decipher what he is saying. He inspects what is presented to him and says something Sam finds unintelligible but Walter seems to understand. Sam has to go into hospital and have what he thinks he hears described as a 'little snip' and which Sam later understands to be a circumcision.

Sam has been in hospital twice before, once to have his belly button fixed as a tiny baby and once with Joy when they both had their tonsils removed. He has vague memories from the second occasion of a man in a white coat standing over him with a gas mask poised over his face before it is laid over his mouth, recollections which still scare him. This time, Sam realises that he must go into hospital on his own and leave Joy at home.

Sam lies alone in a bed with 'Nil by mouth' above him, and the next morning, after he has had to miss out on the Rice Krispies everyone else is eating, a nurse comes to shave the pubic hairs that have recently begun to appear. A smiling doctor comes to see Sam and tells him cheerfully that this is a very minor matter and that after his 'little snip', he will soon be as right as rain. Then Sam lies on a trolley and is wheeled through endless corridors to the operating theatre where he has a 'pre-med', which he is told will make him feel funny and light-headed, and is asked to count down from 10. They are right: Sam is soon out for the count. 10, 9, 8, 7…

Sam comes round feeling dreadful, with a very sore throat and an even sorer willy. This he cannot see because it is bandaged so heavily that it appears to be several times its normal size. After a day or so, he makes it home with Walter and is left to rest for a few days before returning to school. When the doctor calls a day or so later to remove the bandage and redress his wounds, Sam is shocked at the bloody mess he sees. The pain is excruciating and he cannot believe that this, the blood and all the bandages, can mean that all he has had is the little snip he was promised. The truth is that he has been butchered.

Walter is now at work and Sam is being looked after by Marieke and his sisters, Joy and Helen. Sam feels not only very sore but also embarrassed and humiliated about what has been done to him while he was asleep and completely powerless. Sam also feels in his gut that he has been betrayed

Further Up the Beach

by people he trusted, like the doctors who told him it was nothing to worry about. Perhaps this is what adults mean by 'white lies'.

Slowly, very slowly, things improve and the bandages come off and the pain gradually subsides. Now though, Sam sees that he looks different and realises that in fact they have removed some of the skin which had been part of him before.

This experience, along with the earlier memories of the still-baffling talk with his father in the garage about the mysterious seed, as well as the bath time which went so badly wrong, coalesces somehow with the many other exhortations and imperatives from his father that Sam is doing his best to absorb, understand and put into practice. Sam now draws what he believes to be the inescapable conclusion that there is somehow something intrinsically problematic about his own self in general and perhaps about being a boy in particular.

From this point onwards, he resolves to take no more risks which might lead him to further trouble and confusion. Rather than embarking on an exploration of his own body and sexuality, as countless generations of boys have done before and will do in the future, Sam now does what he thinks is safest and instead disavows this fundamental part of himself. Of course, he knows it exists but he sets it aside determinedly, separating and even proscribing it from the rest of himself in a bid to feel safe and secure. It is basically pretty simple and Sam is as certain as he can be that he has arrived at the right formula.

Now though, Sam finds that his fears about red ants, germinating peas and mould on trees continue to multiply and grow. There is little that he cannot conceive of doing to bring harm to either himself or his family, even though he knows in the depths of his heart that he has no desire nor inclination to behave in any of the ways he fears most.

But Sam is drawn to those fears and the convenient and devastating punishments they represent as a moth is drawn inexorably to the light. The punishment is his intricate and perverse creation and he is hooked to it as certainly as the leaves are to the trees and the sun to the sky. Sam thinks back to one of his earliest memories of placing his own pocket money on his father's chest of drawers because he had convinced himself that he had done the worst possible thing in the world and stolen from his father, even though he had not.

Battening all this down is such hard work that it produces in Sam an almost permanent sense of dread in the pit of his stomach, along with an elaborate range of obsessive rituals designed to bring fleeting relief. But, Sam reasons, at least this means that he need not tell a single living soul about the terrifying mystery of what is going on inside his head nor the shame that this makes him feel.

13. THE ROT

When The Beatles first appear on the scene, even Walter seems amused at the way the cheeky lads from Liverpool say 'Thank you very much' lots of times at the end of their first songs. Like the 1966 World Cup Final, these songs find their way into the family's sitting room via their monochrome TV which is disguised as something else when the TV is switched off and its concertina doors are closed.

Walter does not seem to mind The Beatles' early songs either and can even be found tapping his foot sometimes to 'She Loves You' and 'Can't Buy Me Love'. He makes his family laugh when he tells of how he impressed his work colleagues by singing along to The Supremes' big hit 'Baby Love', much to the amazement of his much less 'with-it' colleagues. He can even just about tolerate Donovan's debut single 'Catch the Wind', although he does make clear that he strongly disapproves of the length of this young man's hair.

At this point, there have already been some early warning signs of the more fundamental change that is yet to sweep the country. Bob Dylan's 'The Times They Are a-Changin' has given due warning about how great the challenges ahead might be for Walter and others like him, but perhaps Walter remains blissfully unaware of that particular anthem. He has, however, been aware of Kenneth Tynan's first use of the word 'fuck' on television and joined the public outcry; he also supported Mary Whitehouse's letter to his revered Queen for Tynan the rebel to be reprimanded.

In general, however, Walter still believes that this new pop culture is only a phase, and that short back and sides, along with formal dress, will still rule the world and everything will basically stay the same. Despite what has happened so far, the order of things remains relatively clear. Although National Service has already been abolished, most people's hair is still the kind of short back and sides Walter is used to, AA patrolmen still salute the owner of a car with an AA badge, men usually look like men and women look like women. Young people generally do what they are told and respect for elders is a given, if not as absolute as it once was. Memories of the war, though fading, still live on and Walter does not look out of place as he dresses down at the weekend in his sports jacket, tie and immaculately-pressed flannels.

But the new era does not fade away, and on the back of those songs of the early and mid-1960s come masses of new groups and sounds which suddenly do not seem so innocent to Walter. Marieke loves Peter Noone from Herman's Hermits singing 'There's a Kind of Hush' but Walter counters by saying he is a cissy. He says he cannot stand Donovan now at any price and maybe senses something about his latest song, 'Mellow Yellow', which is not exactly expressing support for the established order.

Further Up the Beach

Although Cilla Black and Dusty Springfield bring brief and welcome respite, Sam starts to see, very slowly but certainly, that all this is beginning to get to his father. Walter can sense something very big, much bigger than him, emerging from the shadows and he does not like it at all.

This is not simply a figment of Walter's imagination. Society is altering dramatically – sometimes, it seems, almost daily – and he is not the only one of his generation to feel intense disquiet. There are always changes across the generations but these are of a different order. It is almost as if the end of the war and the tearing up of ration books has ushered in a weird time warp, as a result of which Walter is having to witness a world which, in more normal circumstances, would be reserved for generations long after his death.

Walter notices that not only are young people starting to dress much more casually than before, but soon they have also moved from casual to downright scruffy. Hair is not only on the collar, but over it, and in no time, chaps are wearing hair down to their shoulders or even their waist and also going unshaven. Casual slacks turn into denims which at first are dark but soon become faded and even bleached, with outrageous bell bottoms which fray at the bottom above open-toed sandals. Young men who would have been fighting and dying in the war not so long ago now do not seem to give a toss for any of that stuff, and instead some even go round wearing beads.

Young people start to see the Queen as an irrelevance at best and patriotism seems to be dead or dying. The whiff of marijuana and rebellion, only a little while ago just a small blot on the landscape, now seems to be everywhere and Walter starts to feel that the world he knew and loved is disappearing fast. What he calls the 'scruff culture' is quickly becoming embedded in the new world and changing beyond recognition all that he has ever known and loved.

Walter develops the theory that the nihilistic chaos now surrounding him amongst the young generation has been triggered by a combination of The Beatles and the abolition of National Service. Together, he decides, they are the forces which have started what Walter calls 'the rot'. The politicians of the day seem to be against poor Walter too. Pipe-smoking Harold Wilson (who does not speak as Walter says Sam must) and Home Secretary Roy Jenkins choose to bring an end to censorship at the theatre, make divorce and abortion easier and take the first steps to bringing homosexuality out of the closet.

Sam wonders whether Walter might be right, that there is a malign force out there against which his father will protect his children and that perhaps he knows more about this than Sam does. Walter, who has never really shaken off the scars of wartime battle, now senses that a new peacetime battle is beginning, every bit as important as the one fought against Germany and Japan. It is now not only a battle against how Sam might speak and behave which could bring upon him shame and humiliation but also a battle against the two fingers Walter feels he is getting from all around him – TV, radio and people on the streets.

In Walter's mind, his own personal battle against 'the rot' and his bid to return the world to what it once was have started. The adrenaline has begun coursing through his body again and he is not going to give up without a hell of a fight. The Hun has already been defeated and so too now must be this new and unexpected enemy which has invaded the country he loves so much.

Top of the Pops is always on TV on Thursday nights and Sam settles down to watch it, wondering what will have climbed the charts and whether he might one day be allowed to look a bit more like some of the stars of the show by having his hair longer. He is not aware of the shift that has been taking place in Walter's mind since he last saw it, that he has started to see all this no longer as a bit of harmless froth but instead, a combination of forces that threaten to change the kind of world he and his mates have fought to preserve.

Which of the effeminate, unpatriotic young men, entirely devoid of talent, flick the switch inside Walter's head on that particular night, Sam does not remember. But he quickly becomes aware of his father's sudden, immense and rapidly mounting anger as he rails against what is being displayed in front of him. He is suddenly loud, domineering and scary. He denounces the permissive society, The Beatles who started all this and the cult of scruffiness which is all around him. Sam screws up every ounce of his courage to say that he likes the music and the groups on *Top of the Pops* but Walter snorts with derision and continues to rant and rave about what is being projected into the family sitting room, loathing and perhaps fearing from the bottom of his heart all that he sees.

The atmosphere is tense because Sam knows there can be only one winner in this kind of situation, that Walter must impose his views and exert his authority on those around him as certainly as if his life depends upon it. Sam feels upset and intimidated to see his father so out of control and also feels that part of his own self is being criticised because these songs are those Sam loves; pop music feels part of him, part of who he is and the person he is becoming. In this way, it feels to Sam that he is also under attack, as well as all those outlandish hairy creatures Walter watches with dismay and disbelief on television.

Walter's rage mounts to such a crescendo that in the end, *Top of the Pops* becomes a sideshow and instead, Sam is watching Walter's meltdown with a sinking feeling of dread in the pit of his stomach. The television is finally switched off amidst bitter recriminations and an uneasy peace descends. There are subsequent attempts to watch it again and although Walter seems to have recovered by the following week, the episode after that reignites his smouldering rage which means that *Top of the Pops* is never watched at home again. Sam decides it is not worth it and that it is easier instead to keep the peace and listen to Alan Freeman's *Pick of the Pops* on Sunday evenings in the bath.

But at the same time, he cannot help hating and resenting his father for having controlled the situation in this way: he feels to Sam to be an out-of-control tyrant who will brook no dissent. Walter has imposed his will on everyone else and got his own way but at the same time, he has made Sam's insides churn even more than they already were. Walter's anthem might have been 'I Won't Back Down' but for the fact that the song had not at that time been released, and anyway, Tom Petty would have sent him into even greater apoplexy. Sam's, on the other hand (and perhaps even Walter's too, had it been stripped of all he detested so much), might have been Tom Petty's 'You Don't Know How it Feels', though again, this followed Walter's death some years later.

Further Up the Beach

Apart from the late-night smacked bottom after lights-out time, Walter still does not hit Sam, but Sam feels nevertheless that he needs to be light on his feet to dodge his father's blows. This is the man who is known to be cheerful, amusing and the proud father of a 'jolly happy family' but it does not feel like that to Sam right now.

Sam continues to lap up all the pop music he can when Walter is not around, and becomes an avid fan of Cat Stevens and Neil Young. They look like Sam would like to look if only he were able to grow his hair, which remains an ever-present source of acrimonious exchange with his father during Sam's adolescent years. Sam's pop star heroes sing about feelings which Sam knows he has deep inside him and would love to express but simply cannot risk doing so.

Walter hears Cat Stevens' track 'Longer Boats' playing and demands to know what the words mean, since, to him, they seem so utterly senseless. Sam cannot explain them in logical, rational terms. He wants to say that their exact meaning may not matter because they mean something to him and make him feel like a message of great importance is being communicated to him and him alone. But Sam cannot find the words to say this, nor begin to be able to understand the feelings they create in him. So he fails to give Walter the explanation his father demands but does not really want. Even if Sam were able to do so, he is feeling more and more intimidated about all this, realising that whatever he says is not going to make the slightest difference to Walter's view of the world. So Walter satisfies himself of the complete worthlessness of these nonsensical lyrics and that he is right to loathe them, as well as the long-haired man who sings them so earnestly.

After numerous further inquisitions of this sort, Walter appears to have a spring in his step. He is making inroads on the new enemy Sam is flirting with and is feeling ever more vindicated about his progress in this direction. The recollections in his own head about how Germany was defeated and how much fortitude and courage that required are again fresh in his mind, despite the passing of two decades, and he feels he must now show that resolve again.

Meanwhile, Sam is feeling more diminished and dominated than ever, increasingly uncertain and anxious about where all this might end and who exactly his father is deep down. Sam, of course, knows nothing of the reality of his father's wartime experiences, nor how these have left their indelible mark on Walter's shattered nerves.

There are moments of respite, such as when Sam is playing the piano and Marieke and Walter come and listen and tell him how beautifully he plays. Sam is not actually particularly good but he loves the pieces his piano teacher chooses for him. Sometimes he cannot make the keys do what he wants them to do and becomes frustrated and angry, hitting them with his clenched fist. Marieke tells Sam he has a temperamental nature and Sam wonders whether she hopes this might point the way to a star-studded future. He dimly realises that this is one of the few occasions he does become angry but it is always with an object rather than a person. Most of the time with his family, Sam is concentrating hard on being the easy-going chap Walter so often comments on because Sam has worked out that this brings him the approval and acceptance he craves.

Other times of peace and harmony during Sam's adolescence are when he sits and watches programmes such as *Yes Minister, Dad's Army* or *The Rise and Fall of Reginald Perrin*, which he and Walter both love. At these times though, it feels to Sam as if he and his father are sitting in parallel universes, both loving in their own ways what they are watching but neither able to communicate across the yawning chasm that separates them. Sam adores Paul Eddington and sees him as a kind of alternative father figure. He is about the right age and seems to be not only kind but also content to show the world that he is uncertain of himself at times, without the unpredictable and irrational outbursts of temper his own father shows from time to time. Sam wonders what it might be like to have a father who could chat with him about his day without reminding him all the time about how he must speak or behave in order to avoid becoming branded.

Sam realises that Walter is a very different man inside than out and that he wears a disguise a lot of the time. It is a very good disguise most of the time and very few people outside their family know he wears it. Perhaps Walter himself does not know because it has become so much a part of him. Sam wonders whether perhaps disguises will be an important way of surviving what life will throw at him in the future. Perhaps, he thinks, he needs to make his own as perfect as that of his father.

14. ANOTHER PLANET

Sam is slippered on his first day at secondary school because he is leaning against a wall, rather than standing up straight whilst waiting to go into a classroom. It stings like crazy but he feels mildly elated that he has been through this unasked-for initiation ceremony so early in his new school career, and receives a welcome boost in admiration from those around him. Sam is the first amongst his friends to have experienced this and they clamour round, demanding to know more, including the size and colour of Mr Kelly's slipper. Sam assumes that Mr Kelly's choice of the slip-on variety, rather than one with laces, increases its suitability for the task by adding to its overall bendiness and this prompts animated discussion amongst the group of new boys.

Classroom teachers are allowed to wield the large black slipper and do so fairly regularly. The cane, however, is reserved to Mr White, the head teacher, who Sam notices pronounces the 'cush' of cushion as rhyming with hush or rush when said by someone from the Home Counties. Sam wonders whether maybe there is something to his father's theories about Lincolnshire accents after all. Mr White has obviously done some serious work on disguising his own, though this has not completely worked to anyone in the know, as Sam is on this particular matter.

It is widely rumoured that, as a prelude to giving the cane, Mr White tells the young boys cowering in front of him that the act of caning them is going to hurt him much more than it will hurt them. Sam has an opportunity to find out more about this curious phenomenon when he is caught throwing snowballs in the playground. Perhaps they have been expressly forbidden to do so because they might contain ice and are considered dangerous, or perhaps no-one has said anything and they have just assumed that snow is there for no other purpose than to be thrown at each other.

Mr White addresses the group of lads in front of him in exactly the way folklore says he does, looking and sounding grave and sorrowful that it has come to pass that he must again be hurt in a way he would not have chosen. Sam and his mates all bend in turn to offer their bottoms, to the delectation of their head teacher whose cane swishes, landing twice with expert precision on each of their backsides. Again, Sam's stock is raised and he walks with a painful swagger and a spring in his step for a few days. Poor Mr White, his pain must be very great indeed.

Sam is popular with his peers but develops into quite a bad boy during this time, always in the same class as Joy and living in her shadow, as she is much more able than her twin brother. They have a lovely French teacher, an elderly motherly soul who is sweet and kind and encourages Sam to enjoy her subject, which he does.

Further Up the Beach

Sam hopes that he might be good at art like his Danish grandfather who became a sculptor, but all the evidence suggests that Sam is actually pretty hopeless and it is soon noted by the art teacher that when he tries to draw people, he frequently forgets to include their arms. This might be because Sam is careless. Or it might be that this says something about his fears deep down that other people's arms, like his father's, could be used to hurt him, were he to change his mind about keeping a stick like Uncle Andrew's. Sam is also often scared of Charles's frequent uncontrolled rages when he loses at something or is bowled out at cricket.

Sam might be worried too that he could use his own arms to hurt and harm someone else, like a member of his own family, in a way he would dread. Then he would no longer be seen as happy, easy-going Sam who always has a smile on his face. But for whatever reason, Sam's drawings of people simply do not have arms.

Sam has a term playing rugby which is completely new to him, but because he is quick, he is told that he could be the best rugby player the school has ever produced. The school is not a rugby-playing school but Sam is pleased nevertheless.

Shortly after this, he finds himself alone during a game with that strange-shaped ball and nothing other than 50 yards between him and touching down a spectacular try which would be talked about for ages and could only enhance his reputation. Sam can hear the sound of heavy breathing behind him, at which point he starts to consider the possibility that he may get caught, and what seems like certain glory will quickly turn into disaster. His legs, which only seconds ago were feeling strong and certain, suddenly feel weak and he is aware of a rising panic in his chest as he attempts to combine running at speed with staying cool inside.

Suddenly the pressure becomes too much to bear and he slings the ball carelessly but decisively behind him to no-one but the muddy ground. The chance is lost and there is general bafflement about what on earth might have led him to squander this most glorious of chances. Sam feels angry and disappointed with himself, but also relieved that the pressure on him has been lifted.

As the final year of three draws to a close, Sam becomes involved in what he is reliably informed is a time-honoured school tradition of snipping off the school ties of those around him and allowing them to do the same to his. This is a celebration of the band of brothers' pending departure from the school, when they will no longer have to wear the blue and white diagonally striped ties they have worn with not much pride for the preceding three years. Perhaps if this had been the last day or the last but one, they would have got away with it, but unfortunately they choose to complete the ritual a week or so before the end of term which is too early for the school's liking.

Again, Sam finds himself in Mr White's office, anticipating another dose of his cane and vowing this time to examine the head teacher's face more carefully to check how deep his sorrow really is. But Mr White takes them all by surprise by issuing instead a fixed-term suspension of one week. Their parents are to be informed, and Sam and his friends will not be returning to school because by the time their exclusion ends, so too will the final term.

Sam leaves the school with two friends and together they feel a sense of elation that they are allowed to wander

Further Up the Beach

the streets and do exactly as they please until home time. But this is tempered by feelings of anti-climax and foreboding as the day draws to a close and they realise they will have to face their parents who are likely to have something to say about all this. The rootless reprobates wander aimlessly round the shops, wondering about doing a bit of shoplifting as they have done before, but calculate correctly that to get caught would only make things worse than they already are.

When Walter hears that Sam has been excluded, he surprises Sam by telling him that cutting off school ties sounds a little like the jolly japes he and his mates used to get up to in the Air Force. His father seems to understand that it was high spirits, rather than any malice, which led to this. For a brief time, it seems that Sam has got away with it completely but that is not quite true. Instead of telling him off for his behaviour, Walter tells Sam that he must do all he can to remember what Walter has told him before about how he must speak and behave, since having this polished veneer is the most important thing for his future and will mean (as Sam knows very well by now) that he will not be branded for his failures in this area.

This is more of the same from Walter, and Sam now understands very well not only how important this is to his father, but how, deep down, Walter is a bit of a rule-breaker, so long as the rules are not his and so long as that essential veneer is firmly in place. Walter often tells his children that he left school without any qualifications and believes that public school-type polish is much more important than passing exams. He also often says how he distrusts experts, as should we all. So, taking everything together, Sam reckons that his father is pretty much the original anti-intellectual.

Sam has a good few days doing stuff other than attending school and even returns one afternoon with Charles to the neighbouring school which Charles attended to play cricket in the nets. Sam wonders whether he is supposed to be doing this but it is good fun and no-one spots that he is supposed to be excluded from the adjacent school premises.

Then Sam and Joy start to attend the brand new school which has just been finished opposite their house where open fields used to be. This bright, shining new school is very modern and experimental, with pupils becoming students and expected to call all teachers by their first names, including Harold, the very trendy head teacher. At first, both resist going, badly wanting to stay with their old friends who will be going elsewhere. But they lose the argument at home because it seems to make sense for them to go to a school so very close to where they live.

Here though, old-fashioned subjects, such as history and geography, are abruptly ousted from the curriculum, to be replaced by sociology, the new, stroppy kid on the block. There is no such thing as English literature, and in two years, Sam does not read a single book. Instead, he does creative writing which amounts to simply being asked to write something from within his own head. It is as if the English teacher thinks the students already know all they need to know and his job is no more than to ask them to write it out, rather than help young people become interested in anything new.

There is a great deal going on in Sam's head but he dare not write any of that down at school because it all makes

Further Up the Beach

him feel so guilty and confused, so instead, he is careful to produce material that will not give anything away.

The general plan at this school is that students learn not because they have to, but instead because they want to. Exams will not be the be-all and end-all. In fact, the number of exams this fodder of the educational revolution will take will be drastically reduced because too many are considered to be nonsensical, and those that remain will be the logical conclusion of having followed and enjoyed a subject for the sake of the subject and not just the exam. Here, they will choose to behave well, not because they will otherwise get caned or slippered, but because to do otherwise will interfere with their learning, as well as that of others. There are plush carpets on the floor and they sit at carousels rather than the old-fashioned desks in rows they are used to.

Sam quickly becomes part of the place and, whatever its faults, develops intense loyalty to the school's ethos and teachers. Walter, in the meantime, having decided Sam and Joy must go there, flips in the opposite direction, quickly becoming fiercely antagonistic to everything that slowly unfurls before his disbelieving eyes.

He develops an unshakeable distrust of François, the French teacher, who is actually quite a traditional teacher but who, during an open evening whilst talking with Walter and Marieke, makes the mistake of scratching intently under his armpits as if there is some living creature nesting there. This apart, Walter is deeply alarmed that sociology may be being used by left-wing teachers to undermine respect for authority, as well as traditional institutions like the monarchy which seems less popular than ever before. Sam dares not tell his father that they also study the sociology of the family and that there are some alternative views about whether the traditional nuclear family is always the best way to raise society's young.

Walter meets Sebastian, an open-toed sandals-wearing sociology teacher, at the family home to discuss the school's approach to students, and reports that his effeminacy makes his flesh creep, rather as Peter Noone from Herman's Hermits does.

Afterwards, Sam asks Sebastian (who insists on being called Seb) how he found meeting his dad. Seb, clearly still shell-shocked from the experience, replies that it was rather like meeting someone from another planet. Sam knows of course that Walter can be narrow, dogmatic and judgemental but feels upset about what Seb has said about him because, Sam thinks, it is one thing for him to think and know this about his father but he is not sure anyone else should.

A damning piece appears in the local paper about how vandalism at the school is going unchecked and how discipline has broken down. Sam rushes to the defence of the school, as, whatever its faults, he now feels part of it, just as it feels part of him. Those who criticise the school are also criticising a part of Sam, just as when Walter criticises the music Sam loves, he is crushing part of who Sam is and wants to be.

Sam realises now that although he cannot seem to draw, he is good with words and feels that it is important to defend something, like an idea or a person, when they are under attack. He would like to use some of these words to express to his father how he feels when Walter does this to him, rather than simply feeling crushed and helpless in the face of his awesome power.

Further Up the Beach

Rather unexpectedly, Sam gets the chance to read out a piece of creative writing along with others at the local radio station which is doing a programme about the school and promises to be more positive than the piece which appeared in the local paper. They sit round a large table, each with a microphone in front of them, and are asked to read their contributions, one after the other. Sam's is about what life was like for people in Copenhagen when it was occupied by the Germans in the Second World War, which Marieke has told her family about, including how much she still hates those 'bloody Jerries'. She tells Sam that they used to creep up behind the German soldiers standing beside the freezing Nyhavn and push them in, then run for their lives, and Sam has worked this into the piece.

After his friend has read the first story, Sam drops a clanger by banging down a glass of water on the table, rather than placing it down very carefully as they have been instructed. It is when they are told that they must re-run this, as it will not go down well when the recorded programme is broadcast, that Sam realises that he has been wrong in his calculation that it would be broadcast live and Walter would therefore miss it because he would be at work.

This poses a new and massive dilemma for Sam – should he continue with his plan to read his piece with the local accent Walter despises but which Sam's classmates expect or should he deliver it in his other 'language' which is spoken at home? He is with his friends who would ridicule him mercilessly if he were to start talking differently from how they normally hear him, so he decides to talk as he always does with them and take a risk about Walter tuning in to the recording at some future date. Sam's turn comes and he reads pretty well. But he wishes that he only had one language to worry about and thinks it would make things much easier for everyone, apart from Walter, if this were the case.

After it is all over, they learn that the programme is likely to be broadcast sometime within the next couple of months. Sam worries about this and, unlike everything else which worries him, he calculates that he can tell someone else. So he tells his older sister Helen of the dilemma. She does not tell Sam not to worry and that it will all be fine, because she knows, like Sam, that if Walter were to hear the programme and learn of Sam's treachery, he would go crazy with anger and disappointment.

It does not occur to Sam that he might also confide in his father and explain what has happened and why he chose to do what he did because Sam knows that there is simply no way he would understand. Sam's dialect, like his haircut and manners, cannot be negotiated, and on matters like this, Sam experiences his father as a frightening despot.

Months go by, during which Sam listens carefully for any signs that the programme might have a date for broadcast, but he hears nothing. In the end, it seems that the programme has already been broadcast and not only Walter but everybody else has missed it, including Sam. So this particular crisis is over, though Sam remains acutely aware of how perilously close to the wind he has sailed and how serious the consequences might have been.

Like most people at Sam's school, he is ill-prepared for the exams which come two years after he started at the school because the idea that they would learn naturally and the exams would take care of themselves has not quite worked out in practice. His German O Level examination is delayed until later that year because the school does not feel confident about how well prepared its students are.

This presents a problem for Sam and Joy because the plan is that by then, they will have moved house from Walter's godforsaken one-horse town to the hallowed South East where he hopes and believes that everything will be much rosier. So Sam and Joy spend time sitting at the old dining table and cluster round Marieke at the head as she teaches them their nominatives and datives so that they are able to take and pass the German exam before they move away in the summer. Sam takes the remainder of his exams and emerges with a total haul of three O Levels, half the number of his much cleverer twin sister, but with identical grades to her for those he does pass.

Sam's crowning glory is an 'ungraded' in maths, which he decided some time ago is a dark art that he simply cannot do. His mind casts back to the exams a couple of months ago and he recalls his decision to walk out of the exam after about 10 minutes, having written little more than his name at the top of the paper. Like his slippering on the first day of secondary school, this unusual result greatly enhances Sam's reputation amongst his friends.

But he reasons that if Walter is right about all this polish stuff, he might be able to get away with not passing many exams, just as he got away with being involved in that tie-snipping incident at his previous school. Instead, he needs to keep working at being as polished as he possibly can, keep hidden the things that trouble him and continue to pretend to be easy-going, relaxed Sam.

Walter tells Sam that it is best to be an extrovert like he is, rather than an introvert, which he makes sound like something very negative. Sam convinces himself that if he can keep all this up, everything will come right in the end. He works on his disguise, just as Walter must have done on his own in the previous decades. In the meantime, Sam's checking that taps are off and that his hands are scrupulously clean continues apace.

But no-one in the world, absolutely no-one, must know about this. Nor must Sam reveal the intense fragility he feels at the core of his soul. He is just about managing to hold all this together, though sometimes he is not sure exactly how.

15. SOUTHBOUND

Once the exams are over, Sam begins to believe what he has known for some time, which is that the whole family is moving house. They are going to live in Godalming in the rolling hills of Surrey, near where Walter was stationed during the war and of which he has vivid memories. This is the place where Walter experienced his humiliation in the officers' mess but also where he learnt the complex, combined arts of polish and disguise as social lubricants. It is also the place this callow youth came of age as a handsome young hero in the cockpit of the Lancaster he piloted so courageously. Walter has never made any secret of loathing the only place Sam has ever called home, nor of his wish to get away from the Lincolnshire accents that surround him and his children every day.

But Sam has lived in this house all his life and so it is a part of him, which means that he does not want to move and nor does Joy. His older brother Charles and older sister Helen are off and away to university by this time and Walter and Marieke have waited until Sam and Joy have completed their exams to make the move.

Walter is keener than ever to move now that he has had the shocking experience of meeting Sam's trendy, progressive teachers at his latest school. They have only reinforced for him his belief that the rot, begun by The Beatles a few years ago, has now well and truly set in. His memories of Godalming during the war are so vivid and his hatred of Lincolnshire so intense that in his mind, Godalming becomes a kind of Mecca. A place where perhaps the rot has not yet reached, and even if it has, where at least people will speak as they are supposed to and perhaps show more respect for things as they were. Walter will be back in the South East where he feels he belongs, whereas Sam and Joy will be separated from all their friends, including their greatest friend, Neil.

Neil has long hair down to his shoulders, as Sam would like to have, and looks like one of the pop stars Walter detests with all his heart and soul. Neil is not rude when he meets Walter but neither is he in the slightest bit polite or deferential, choosing instead to treat Sam's father as more of an equal than an elder. Walter sees in him a thinly-disguised lack of respect, bordering on youthful insolence, and in many ways, Neil is the incarnation of all that he loathes. This vindicates his and Marieke's decision to make the move, which becomes possible because of Walter's change of job.

The crates are packed and loaded onto the lorry parked in the family's drive. The family's large house has been bought, ironically, by Seb, the teacher to whom Walter has taken a particular dislike and who describes Walter as having come from another planet. The house quickly becomes a shell, the contours of which Sam knows like the back of his hand and will never forget.

Further Up the Beach

His bedroom, shared with Charles until the arguments became too ferocious and where Walter many times spotted Sam's light on when he took Teddy for his last walk, prompting him to administer the 'lights out' smacked bottom.

Marieke and Walter's bedroom, where Sam used to lie adoringly on his father's chest when he was tiny, where the family gathered on birthdays for cards and presents and where as a small boy Sam repaid Walter the loose change he feared he might have stolen but had not.

The bathroom, the scene of Sam's innocent prank and his mother's rejection of him and the source of his intense shame.

The wide staircase, whose bend Sam has cheated many times by clambering over the banisters, landing lightly on his feet before descending the rest two at a time.

The dining room, around whose table the children's hungry bellies have been fed, where Sam has been instructed repeatedly and urgently about the importance of polish, manners and speech and where Walter has so often forgone second helpings in favour of his beloved children. Where Walter has created a hatch to the adjoining kitchen and joked about the house falling down and where they have played family games of Monopoly and table tennis.

The kitchen, with its black and white stone floor and separate pantry where Sam has cut many illicit knobs of butter before dunking them in the sugar bowl and placing them delightfully on his tongue, as well as thieving countless squares of raw red jelly.

The sitting room, with windows at both the front and the back, where they have played Happy Families, whist and rummy, where Sam has driven his remote-control car and where each year the family has had a magnificent floor-to-ceiling Christmas tree with lights that sometimes do not work and drive Walter completely mad. This is also where Walter has railed terrifyingly against *Top of the Pops* and placed himself once again on a wartime footing to defeat the new enemy from within.

The patio step, where Sam has sat shelling peas with his sisters Joy and Helen and brother Charles, and first saw red ants escaping from the cracks in their hordes.

The outhouse, whose flat roof Sam has scaled via the bathroom window and whose drainpipe he has slid down whilst practising his heroic boyhood exploits.

The wooden garage, in which he has acted as Walter's worshipping carpentry apprentice and also received instruction in the peculiar facts of life.

The top lawn, where all the children have had such fun running through the sprinkler on boiling hot days and lined up for photos, each of them with their bikes bought and lovingly maintained by Walter. To which poor Teddy has been banished, when he has suddenly and alarmingly transmogrified into his most mysterious 'excited' state.

The vegetable patch, which Marieke and Walter have weeded and then nurtured to help keep their children well fed and where Marieke says she loves being in contact with the soil.

The sports patch, where Sam has learnt to kick a football, throw and catch a tennis ball, hold a cricket bat and whack a shuttlecock. Where also he first saw the woolyafus growing on the trees, in his mind a malignant force which threatened not only his existence, but also that of his whole family.

Further Up the Beach

Although Sam hates the idea of going, it is impossible not to get excited about what is happening. They head down to Godalming where they stay the night in a local hotel opposite a great big patch of green. Sam has never stayed in a hotel before, as the only time they go away is to go on holiday to Scotland or Denmark where they usually rent a house.

In the morning, they drive to their new home which, like the old one, is detached and has a great big garden which is squarer than the one they have just left. The lorry is unpacked and slowly they settle into their new home, with Walter already talking about how it is reminding him of being there during the war and celebrating his long-awaited return to home territory.

Slowly, very slowly, Sam realises something is wrong. Not only does he wish he was still at his old house with all his friends nearby, he is also feeling that something else is missing and has not been taken account of. It is not dear Teddy who is getting old now but is still interested enough to sniff the place enquiringly for new smells. What it is exactly dawns on Sam as he examines the workshops which replace the big wooden garage they had in the home they have left and where Sam used to keep his treasured bike.

Sam's bike! He races round all the unpacked crates and the now-empty lorry but can see no sign of it. Somehow he has become separated from his beloved bike which has failed to make the journey with them. Or rather, they have somehow failed to bring it with them. Sam's bike remains in the place where they used to live, where he still desperately wants to be. Maybe this is all deeply subliminal and there is a piece of this reluctant young immigrant to the South East that has knowingly left it there so that he can maintain a connection with his true home. But reality dawns on Sam and he knows he has no option but to tell Walter.

Walter is cross, understandably so, as it turns out that, for some inexplicable reason, Sam left his bike at a friend's home the night before they left. Arrangements are made for it too to make the move to the family's new home and Sam is thrilled to see it reappear a few days later. But the bike is now quite old and Godalming is hillier than Lincolnshire, so not so good for cycling.

Over the years, Sam has cleaned and polished his bike until it gleamed and Walter noticed the love and care Sam was lavishing on it, but this has not helped Sam expunge the many worries in his head, which are now more entrenched than ever. So Sam sells his bike and he and Joy walk to their new sixth-form college where they are to take A Levels, after teachers at Sam's previous go-ahead school write to say that he is actually quite bright and his measly haul of O Levels a couple of months earlier does not reflect his true abilities.

Sixth-form college proves to be the opposite of Sam's previous school. Teachers suddenly become known as lecturers, and in English, they are fed a diet of mind-numbing note-taking about *King Lear* and *Paradise Lost* by an elderly white-whiskered bore whose mantra is that the college is like a sausage factory and it is his job to turn out well-shaped sausages.

Just nine months after the family's move, Sam hears urgent voices and movement in the middle of the night and wakes bleary-eyed to find Walter being taken downstairs on a stretcher into a waiting ambulance. He learns that Walter has had a massive coronary and may die. Part of Sam

Further Up the Beach

desperately wants his father to live but part of him dares to wonder whether, if he were to die, the sense of life-long oppression that burns bright in the core of his being might be somehow relieved. Sam feels that whatever he does can never please his father and is aware that he is seen by Walter as an integral part of the 'rot' which makes his father so desperately unhappy.

Walter survives, but only just, and Sam celebrates with the rest of the family the miracle of modern drugs, as well as Walter's fortitude, which has made this unlikely outcome possible.

At last, Sam achieves academic success in the form of three very good A Levels and now has to decide what to do next. He tells Marieke that he may not want to go to university as Charles and Helen have already done, and she looks very worried about what might become of him instead. Walter has suggested Sam should have his hair cut and go on a short service commission with the RAF where he could learn to fly a helicopter and have the time of his life.

Neither option seems right to Sam but in the end, he goes to university to study history, simply retracing Charles's steps before him, even though his knowledge of the subject is sketchy and his interest almost non-existent.

Sam learns to drive and quickly finds another irresistible hook for his anxiety as he becomes morbidly preoccupied by a fear of being unable to control the balance of the clutch and accelerator. This carries with it the threat of being 'found out' and therefore humiliated amongst his new friends in Godalming. This fear recedes in time, only to be replaced by many others Sam's ever-active imagination is capable of creating and nurturing for his own pain and penance.

David Monk

Soon he passes his driving test but has a couple of scrapes in Marieke's car in embarrassingly quick succession, which prompt Walter to ground their youngest son whilst he cools down and before anything worse happens. Walter calls this one to perfection, and, though Sam is angry, this is mostly with himself and he respects Walter's decision, which shows wisdom and great judgement.

By the time Sam goes to university, it is clear that Walter is disappointed with the way Godalming has turned out 30 years after the war. He finds that here too are all the hallmarks of the 'scruff culture', which saddens and angers him still more, only adding to his general angst and discontent with the world. The seeds of decay have spread far and wide and remain loathsome and alien to poor, distressed Walter. He tells his family bitterly that this new world is most certainly not the reason he and his comrades fought and died in the war as they did.

The country is going to the dogs in other ways too. Ted Heath is Prime Minister. His shoulders go up and down when he laughs, but there seems little to laugh about and he seems quite unable to control the miners, as Walter says he must. Walter's anger turns to shame when power cuts become a frequent occurrence and the family has to send to Denmark, who depended on us during the war, for a supply of candles to be able to see what they are doing in their own home. What has become of the country Walter loved so much and which used to rule the world?!

Sam returns with Joy to the family's old house just before he goes to university and finds that trendy Seb has made it more modern, but it remains the same shell. Then Sam hears a couple of years later that it is to be demolished

Further Up the Beach

to make an access road to a new estate of houses to be built on the fields at the back – their double-fronted house is the widest in the road and therefore the developer's choice. Sam wonders whether he should go back to see it for one last time but by now he is at university and it seems unimportant.

The bulldozers do not hang around for him to change his mind and the next time Sam goes back, he sees their old neighbours' houses on either side of the brand new road which now runs the length of where his own house used to be and beyond.

Although from now it can exist only in Sam's own mind, his memories of it become sharper and more deeply-rooted than ever. This is the place where Walter and Marieke's family turned complicated and the sense of dread going round endlessly in Sam's head was created and flourished. Sam returns to his current life but knows deep down that there is a mystery to all this which one day he must come to understand.

16. UP HIGH (2)

Now Sam really is up high, higher than ever before and much higher than the tree he scaled in the family's front garden all those years ago. The tiny Cessna is crowded and noisy and he does his best to settle down and stay calm.

His thighs touch those of his parachuting mate Zach as they both crouch down in the back, with Bob the jumpmaster, and the pilot, who seems to have no name and not much conversation, in the front. Bob's craggy, weather-beaten face looks across at them and he gives a big wink. Perhaps this is meant to be reassuring to them as first-timers, or it might just as easily mean he is quite looking forward to pushing them both out of the aeroplane when the moment comes, which will be quite soon.

Sam is not sure whose idea parachuting was but here they are anyway. Less of the training and exactly what he is supposed to do sticks in his mind than he would like, and they have already had a few abortive jumps because of bad weather. He looks across at Zach and for the first time notices his wiry hair and beard, which remind Sam of a little rough-haired terrier. Beneath that, Sam senses an ease and confidence in his mate and guesses that his bowels may not be turning to water quite as his own are.

On their backs are the main parachutes which will be attached to the aeroplane by a static line by the time they make their leap, meaning both will open automatically so that they are able to get back to the safety of the university bar and its cheap beer. On their fronts are the smaller emergency chutes with red handles which they will need to pull if the ones on their backs fail to open automatically. Sam wonders how difficult this might be if he were to find himself hurtling down to earth with nothing else to stop his fall. But he is not really worried about this, as they have been reassured that the main ones almost always open as they should.

Sam has never actually flown before, so this is his first time in an aeroplane. As he peers through the open doorway at the front, he sees the fields and buildings shrinking as they ascend, the cars now no more than glinting specks of silver in the bright sunlight. He shifts his weight on his haunches and tries to look cooler than he feels.

They are jumping from around 2500 feet, which they have worked out is equivalent to more than 400 people of Sam's size standing on top of one another. They have already been to the top of the tallest tower they can find on the university campus to get used to the feeling of being up high. Here, they catch sight of the distant Dales but decide that the real thing will feel different, which it does. And of course this is much, much higher.

Sam is reminded of diving from the top board at his local swimming baths when he was younger, how petrified he felt but how he needed to do it to show his father how brave he was. No-one in Sam's family ever got close to performing this feat, so that act, like parachuting, promised to make him different and unique and would be a way of showing Walter the extent of his youngest son's courage. Sam hopes deep down that this might help make up for some of the other things he feels Walter is dissatisfied with, like who Sam is, how he speaks and dresses, and his lack of polish.

Bob starts mouthing something to them and Sam realises he is telling them he has attached the static lines to the plane. He and Zach both have to pull them to satisfy themselves that this has been done, so Sam gives his a tug and signals a thumbs-up in Bob's direction.

The moment for exit is quickly getting closer, and in Sam's head, he is going over exactly what they have learnt about exiting the plane from its hole in the side. The first is to maintain a star shape, with an arched back, his head clearly focused on the disappearing plane and the whites of the jumpmaster's eyes.

The second is to count out loud as he falls. Not so simple as '1, 2, 3, 4, 5, 6,' but instead, 'One thousand and one! One thousand and two! One thousand and three!' Each represents approximately one second and means that he should be able to judge how long he has been falling and when to reach for the red handle on his front if the worst has happened and his main parachute has not opened. This would be very important if he and Zach were ever to progress to free fall, where no static line is involved and they would have to be able to open their own parachutes at exactly the right time.

Sam is closest to the doorway and so will jump first. Bob points at the doorway and makes an unmistakable gesture in Sam's direction that it is time to go. As Sam edges closer to the door, he has a glorious moment of clarity about what he is required to do to exit the plane in the way he has been taught.

He edges forwards until he is level with the open doorway. As the plane slows, he unfolds his bent right leg from beneath him and places it carefully on the wheel of the plane, which is to act as a step and has been locked into position. Next, his right hand reaches out to grip the strut beneath the wing, followed by his other hand. Sam notices the rivets that hold the strut to the wing and marvels briefly at how they stay connected, despite the intense vibration caused by the engine. The last piece of the jigsaw is his left leg, which, quivering like jelly, he forces to leave the plane to join his right foot on the wheel, each jostling for space, as it is scarcely wide enough to take the width of both. Then he takes his right foot off the wheel and extends it outwards so that he is now in the shape of a star.

Finally, now completely outside the plane but looking in, Sam waits for the signal from Bob. The engine cuts completely for a few seconds and then the promised dig in the ribs materialises, clear, firm and unmistakable, accompanied by a bellowing in his left ear to jump. He does so and hears the plane's engine roar back into life as it disappears into the distance and Sam hurtles towards the ground. His heart is in his mouth as he drops like a stone for a few seconds before hearing the whoosh of his main parachute open above him. His speed of descent slows and Sam realises that, although he is going to be safe, he has completely forgotten to count or make any attempt to maintain his star shape, his limbs splaying unceremoniously in all directions and his first 'One thousand and one' followed by inarticulate screams of joy and terror.

But the feeling of exultation and release is magnificent and all Sam cares about. He wonders how the thrill he has just experienced compares with that of hitting the high spot between the sheets, or anywhere else on terra firma for that matter. He is now at university but, despite having had fleeting girlfriends over the last couple of years, he continues to disclaim the full extent of his sexuality, as he concluded in his adolescent years he must. At this stage, he has not begun to understand the complex combination of forces that have created in him this overwhelming sense of prohibition and obligation, nor the crucial importance of past generations in helping, unintentionally, to pull these levers. He knows that one day this will change, but in the meantime, he continues determinedly to bury the power and desire that exist deep within him.

As he tumbles through the air, then slows as his parachute takes control of his fall, Sam achieves an exhilarating escape from some part of himself he desperately needs to leave behind. This will surely help him feel good about himself and redefine who he is. It will flush from his system the constant feeling of fragility in his innermost core, push away the agitated, noisy butterflies in the pit of his stomach and strengthen his wobbly legs. This is worse when he has been home for the weekend and has to re-enter the crowd at university, and then gets slowly better after he is feeling accepted again into the fold with his university mates over a game of table football.

This is what he knows by now is called free-floating anxiety, which is now with him nearly all the time, its path having been so expertly paved by his earlier fears about stealing Walter's loose change, those red ants crawling from the patio slabs, the dried peas which threatened to germinate inside his head and the dreaded woolyafus on the trees where he loved to play as a child.

Sam's landing on a concrete runway which he has mistaken for the white plastic target cross he is supposed to be aiming for cannot dampen his thrill. As he picks himself up, gathering together his crumpled parachute and rubbing his sore knees which have scraped along the concrete, he is already thinking about which phone box to use to make the call that evening.

He has done it! He has been brave, as Walter was when he jumped from his burning aeroplane over enemy territory during the war. Sam hopes this will help him lay to rest everything that has plagued him for so long and will mean that he can now look forward to the future with a greater certainty of his own worth.

After dinner, he speaks with Marieke, who always sounds more foreign on the phone than in the flesh. She turns the television down to hear Sam's news. She tells him how well he has done, then offers to wake Walter who is asleep in front of the television because he is still not well after his heart attack and is working too hard. There is a queue forming outside the booth, so Sam asks her to tell Walter about the jump and promises to phone again soon. They chat a bit more but before he rings off, he urges her again not to forget to tell Walter. Not only has his act of bravery been performed, but his father will very shortly

Further Up the Beach

know about it. Sam has done all he can for now and cannot wait to see his father again and look him in the eye as his equal for the very first time in his life.

But the glorious feeling of a new Sam, one with whom Sam himself feels happy, lasts only a few days and, like the top board diving, the thrill soon fades and he is left feeling just the same as he did before. He no longer worries about red ants or woolyafus, but instead feels like his insides will crack and break at any point and everything he is working so hard to keep hidden will suddenly pour out.

Sam realises that, although he has jumped from an aeroplane with a parachute, this is nothing to what Walter did before he was born. He wonders how he could ever have thought it possible to compare the two and this reinforces his own acute sense of failure, crushing anonymity and worthlessness. He is back to being the old Sam before he knows it. Perhaps he needs to make another jump and this will do the trick. But deep down, Sam realises that no amount of parachuting is going to sort all this out and instead, the answer lies elsewhere.

17. LOVE AND AFFECTION

Sam first meets Hattie when she is chairing an evening university history society meeting. She tells the assembled company that she is from the law faculty, which explains to Sam why he has never spotted her before. His own attendance at the event is something of a mystery because, although he is studying history, he does not know a great deal about it and it holds no particular interest for him at this time.

He hears Hattie saying in a beautifully modulated tone something like, 'It's been a very interesting evening, but it may be best if we take any further questions in the pub.' Her perfectly-formed words fall from her luscious lips to form the sweetest melody known to mankind, and her deep blue sparkling eyes and captivating smile complete Sam's absolute enchantment.

Hattie, Sam and assorted others go to the pub on the corner, one not known for its style but well-known to the student population. They talk, Sam buys Hattie a drink and falls immediately head over heels in love with her. They start going out within days of that first meeting. Sam sometimes sees Hattie in the library, where she draws a heart on his folder with both their names under it, which he treasures.

Joan Armatrading has her first hit single at this time, called 'Love and Affection'. It is a new and very different sound to what has gone before and resonates with the unique feeling the early days of the relationship evoke in Sam. He has none of the doubts about being in love which Joan Armatrading sings about. Sam walks tall and proud as he and Hattie amble across the road from the library to the refectory, hand in hand. Sam wonders whether this can be real or whether perhaps he is dreaming. This stunning young woman is holding the clammy hand of a gawky youth whose veneer of polish is thinner than she can imagine. Not only that, she seems to be enjoying it.

Other people see them together and slowly the reality dawns on Sam – they are officially 'together' and he is in heaven. Sam loves Hattie's poise and the deep, secure confidence that radiates from a place deep within her. Her long blond hair cascades over her delicate shoulders and sometimes she winds its thick strands absent-mindedly around her little finger as she ponders what is in her doubtless beautiful mind. Her cheekbones are high and she walks with a straight back, often with jeans tucked strikingly into knee-length brown boots. She has a lovely way of giggling and smiles easily and effortlessly. Her chuckle and smile are enough to make Sam go weak at the knees, which is a frequent occurrence.

Hattie speaks with the kind of accent Sam's father urged him to adopt while Sam was growing up, which was difficult because no-one around Sam spoke like that, apart from

Further Up the Beach

Walter. He and Hattie laugh about different regional accents and Hattie's beautiful Home Counties' pronunciation. Hattie comments to Sam with her lovely smile that there is something about his accent which is 'not *quite* southern'. To Sam, her accent is not in the least bit affected or snooty, just completely natural. Although Hattie is human and therefore imperfect, to Sam she is, quite simply, faultless.

Early on, they are kissing and cuddling in Sam's room in his hall of residence where the walls are adorned with pictures of parachuting, the earlier ecstasy of Sam's university career. He is fondling Hattie's breasts under her green, woollen polo neck jumper. She looks directly at him, smiles that captivating smile and suggests it would be easier if she were to remove her top.

After this, he finds it more impossible than ever to contain his excitement at being with her, and sometimes she is disconcerted by his passion and intensity, as well as his unshakeable sense of her as representing something very close to complete perfection. He knows that a lighter touch would be wiser but he finds that impossible because of what she very quickly comes to mean to him.

Sam and Hattie develop an intimate relationship which often far exceeds the early cherished moments with the abandoned green polo neck jumper. He also stays the night with her on several occasions. But it is not as intimate as Sam craves, as, despite early promise, she resists making love, instead urging Sam to 'rise above' his passionate and single-minded desire that they should do so.

Sam finds Hattie's resolve on this issue to be made of the sternest possible stuff, and despite the words of Joan Armatrading's hauntingly beautiful song ringing in their ears, she steadfastly refuses to be persuaded otherwise. Hattie is Catholic, has attended a convent school and has highly-protective parents to whom she feels she must account for her behaviour and decisions. Central to her values and beliefs is that she must retain her 'purity' for later marriage.

However, the boundaries she sets for their intimacy over the many months of their relationship eventually become a destructive bone of contention between them. To Sam, who has battened down sexual desire for this chosen moment for reasons of his own, this all seems rather one-way, not really natural and in no real sense a preservation of innocence, in view of all that he and Hattie do together. He does everything within his power to show her the strength of his feelings for her and the turmoil she is creating but the boundaries remain as immoveable as ever.

Not only can Sam not rise above all this as Hattie exhorts him to do, her eyes shining bright with evangelical resolve, neither can he bring himself to walk away because his leaden feet simply feel too full of crazy love and adoration to do so.

Sam's sense of Hattie's perfection is fuelled by his own glaring sense of his own shortcomings, which he has carried with him for as long as he can remember. They go to see 10cc, famous for the song 'I'm Not in Love', in concert. Sam wonders and worries that perhaps Hattie might be saying that to him but hopes and prays that this is not the case. They go to see a one-day cricket match when the weather gets warmer, and Hattie suffers terribly because of hay fever. Her eyes and nose stream without end and eventually she has to give up and go home. She looks dreadful, but to Sam, she remains lovelier than ever.

Sometimes they talk about looks and Sam tells Hattie what he thinks of her and asks her what she thinks of him. She giggles and says, very affectionately, that he is 'funny-looking'. That is fine by Sam because she is happy to be seen with him and enjoys his company, so that is all that matters.

Hattie wears glasses for some things, which make her look a bit more like the barrister she hopes to become. During the time they are going out together, Sam has to start wearing glasses too and he goes through agonies that she might reject him when he dares to produce them. But she does not, much to Sam's eternal relief, and he loves her all the more for that.

They visit each other's homes during holidays and Sam proudly parades Hattie to Walter, Marieke and his brother and sisters. Walter likes the way she speaks and Sam feels she is a big hit with his father for this, if for no other reason. Hattie is with Sam's family when they visit friends of Walter and Marieke. Hattie explains to them who she is and how she knows Sam and his family. As she does so, Sam marvels at her sense of self-assurance in a strange environment and wonders where she has acquired her own unique brand of glittering polish.

Sam visits Hattie's family home three times, the first around his 21st birthday. Hattie comes to see him in his separate bedroom to give him his presents and Sam's heart gives a lurch in anticipation of where this might lead. But then he is appalled to see her mother follow closely behind, obviously with no intention of letting her precious daughter spend time alone here with Sam. Sam aches for her to do so, his cock hard with desire, and his head now feeling entirely free of guilt because he knows in his heart of hearts that this is who and what he has been waiting for over the many years of his suppressed desire.

On the same visit, he becomes aware that Hattie's father is a keen follower of rugby. Hattie is an only child and so the mantle of keeping her father company in this passion has fallen squarely to her. Sam notices a loving bond between the two, and that when she talks with her father about rugby, the twinkle in her sparkling eyes seems to shine brighter than ever. Sam realises pretty quickly that he will need to mug up on all this, as all he knows about is football.

Sam is asked by Hattie's parents over an early Saturday evening drink what he is planning to do when he leaves university. He has no idea why he is at university and even less clue as to what he might choose to do when he leaves and so he shrugs and replies gracelessly that he has not the foggiest idea. He registers surprise and perhaps concern from Hattie's parents, as his own evident lack of future direction contrasts sharply with their daughter's already well-mapped-out career.

Sam is at Hattie's home over Easter and together they watch Red Rum triumph in the Grand National. They watch the race from an old folks' home, where Hattie's grandfather is living his last sad days. During the same stay, they play tennis and Hattie becomes cross with Sam for not playing his part in getting the rallies going. Sam is guilty as charged but his mitigation is that he is concentrating more on the madonna at the other end of the court, and in particular, the distraction caused by the contrast of Hattie's pure white skirt with her shapely, tanned legs, most of all as she bends to retrieve the balls at her end of the court.

Hattie eventually decides, after many months, that enough is enough and writes to Sam after he has graduated to tell him it is all over. The letter arrives at his parents' house. Sam picks it up as he arrives home from his summer job as a dustman which has made him fit, strong, tanned and often rather smelly.

After the most cursory of washes, he flies immediately into Marieke's ageing, battered Mini and races from Godalming to the wilds of even leafier Kent to Hattie's home. Sam is very lucky to arrive in one piece. Hattie is working in a pub at lunchtimes and he catches her just as she is leaving to walk home. She is shocked to see him, and clearly Sam has spoilt the rather more clinical ending her letter had intended.

It is a hot summer day. Sam gives her a lift back to her house and they talk for a while. He begs her not to leave him, tells her he loves her and cannot do without her. His love for her is set against her affection for him. She is in tears, but nevertheless stays resolute and firm. Not open to persuasion. Eventually, Hattie opens the car door and heads into her house, saying goodbye to devastated Sam for ever.

Sam urgently seeks help from a joint elder statesman university friend who contacts Hattie on his behalf to check whether there is even a scintilla of doubt in her mind about her decision. Sam cannot believe or accept that he has lost this fair-skinned princess whose beauty and poise he always believed could compensate for his own many imperfections.

His friend writes to Sam afterwards, quoting extracts from Hattie's response, which includes something about Sam's impulsiveness in coming to see her when he had received her letter announcing the end of their relationship. This last throw of the dice has failed. It is over.

Sam tells his family the news in the most abbreviated form but his anguish is so great that he cannot bring himself to talk about it properly with them or anyone else, having learnt the tricks of self-survival and disguise. Instead, he does what he has already done with so much else and buries this still-weeping pain alongside the myriad other unresolved feelings from his earlier past. Now he decides that the smile he shows to the outside world must be even bigger and broader than ever.

***

His smile flatters the girl at the party. She has drunk cheap gin, and Sam is tipsy on several pints of Watney's Red Barrel. Seamlessly, they move from chatting and gently rubbing thighs on the faux leather settee to the pristine comfort of her parents' bed, where Sam is struck by the pungent smell of her mother's perfume.

She is no slouch and urges Sam to move with the same speed before they are missed downstairs. But Hattie's face appears again, as do all the convoluted contours from his earlier past. He tries to erase them from his mind, but they refuse to vanish or even fade from view.

His companion loses patience and scoots out of bed as quickly as she fell into it, leaving Sam in a drunken reverie of past and present, accompanied by the beat of the Moody Blues below. It is only as he hears the closing of the door that he realises he still does not know her name.

18. I BELIEVE IN YOU

Now Sam is in Oxford, training to be a history teacher. He knows almost nothing about history before 1945 but is hopeful that he might get away with this if he mugs up on the many other centuries, which are pretty much a blank as a result of his unusual education. Even though it is not necessary for the syllabus, he buys a couple of simple books, such as *Kings and Queens of Great Britain*, to try to make up for the yawning gaps in his knowledge of past events.

The first few weeks of the new term present no threat to this budding history teacher almost entirely bereft of historical knowledge. The days are bathed in warm autumn sunshine and lectures get off to a slow start, which makes Sam and those around him feel as if they are still on summer holiday.

He has largely funded this year at university by working a third summer as a dustman, where he is reminded by middle-aged colleague Fred to always remember the twin adages that his own mother taught him, which were that 'courtesy costs nothing' and that 'the pen is mightier than the sword'.

Sam meets Chloe at the Grad Pad where Saturday night discos are held and they all get drunk. She is a great dancer; her eyes shine and sparkle with a mixture of fun, mischief and defiance. She is a rebel with a terrific, athletic body of which she is proud and which draws many male (and perhaps female) eyes to her. She exudes a strong sense of self which makes her forthright and confident.

She is unlike Sam's previous girlfriend Hattie in so many ways, but most of all in that she is not in the least bit holy or rigid about sex. Hattie, with whom Sam was madly in love until she consigned him to her past only months ago, left Sam feeling bruised, battered and confused. Chloe, on the other hand, has had lots of boyfriends and has no hangs-ups whatsoever about all this.

They are dancing to Cockney Rebel's 'Make Me Smile (Come Up and See Me)', and Chloe is making clear in her animal way that she is up for sex with Sam as they dance together against a background haze of alcohol, Grad Pad strobe lighting and general student mayhem. Back in her shared house, fucking does not work the first time or the second, but once she realises the score, she sorts it out and Sam achieves the magnificent big O, the first time in his waking life that this has ever happened.

The dam has burst its banks with a thunderous roar after only a few moments on an otherwise peaceful Oxford night. However, its debris remains and will only be dredged to the surface, brick by brick, when Sam is much older.

Meanwhile, Chloe tells Sam that he is like a cat that has had the cream and they carry on doing the natural healthy thing of screwing good and often. Sometimes this is in her cosy bedroom a short cycle ride away from the city centre and at other times at her parents' home, where she has the luxury of a double bed, and they move in rhythmic unison to the sound of her favourite Steve Miller Band's 'Fly Like an Eagle' vinyl. At others, they park one of their old Minis up at the garages, where they perform feats of athleticism reserved for the young and highly flexible creatures they are.

At last, Sam can feel confident that he is not doing anything wrong; all this is not only okay, but also right and natural. But so much has gone before, it is not always plain sailing from here. Occasionally, he goes off the boil but she helps him reset his mind and then they are back on track. At last, he has permission to behave as a fully-fledged male sexual creature.

Sam does not tell Chloe about all that has happened before, mainly because, at this point of his life, he has not begun to work it out. But he does tell her briefly about holy Hattie and Chloe listens with refreshing astonishment about how any self-respecting girl could behave in the way she did. As he tells Chloe, he cannot believe that he loved, waited and hoped as he did, but that is all history now.

They cannot have sex all the time, so sometimes they stay in the college bar and drink with friends. Much of this is free because Sam and a couple of mates work behind the bar and stocktaking is lax, as are their financial scruples. At other times, things are more mundane and they meet in the laundry of the post-graduate college where they are based or in a coffee shop, where they drink mugs of hot chocolate as the weather gets colder.

Sometimes, Chloe has to stay in, surrounded by mountains of books with mysterious titles. She is training to be an accountant and the texts she studies make Sam's head spin in admiration and disbelief.

Chloe powers her way round town on a green racer and Sam rides his motorbike which he has brought from home. He gives her many illegal rides after nights out, hoping that neither his L plates nor his alcoholic breath will give him away. Sam is adopted by Chloe's female housemates who make Sam feel thoroughly at home and spoilt. Together they all go to a fancy dress ball, with Sam as a sheik, complete with harem. This means that Sam spends only very little time in his own digs a short ride away. Once, he leaves his little red cigarette-making machine at her house and the next day finds it sitting on the seat of his motorbike, together with a cheeky note from this tasty lady.

They hire punts from Magdalen Bridge and learn to punt down the Cherwell, gazing with wonder at the beauty of the bridges and the grandeur of the colleges. Chloe's mum and dad visit for the weekend and bring her kid sister, who is intensely curious about her older sister's latest boyfriend and casts many surreptitious glances in Sam's direction while his attention is elsewhere.

Her family seems to Sam to be very different from his own, with Chloe's father in particular appearing ultra-relaxed and as happy to observe as to contribute to what is going on around him. Chloe's family may not agree about everything but there do not seem to be any obvious points of conflict.

Chloe meets Walter for the first time when he fetches Sam at the end of term. Walter is garrulous and extrovert with Chloe and her friends and no-one would guess what might be lurking just beneath the surface of this charming middle-aged man. Sam feels disloyal but tells Chloe afterwards that what you see with his father is sometimes not what you get. In subsequent years, she finds out what Sam is talking about when Walter's mask slips in her presence, and Sam is relieved at least that she has seen it and so does not think he is making it all up.

They go to the Magdalen May Ball, for which Chloe dresses up and looks stunning. Sam sulks terribly for no good reason and manages to upset Chloe to the point of tears. This is what it is intended to do, of course, even though the real target is somebody or something from Sam's childhood which he has not even begun to understand. In the morning, they all punt up the river for breakfast and take photos. Chloe appears in one with her arm round Sam and her head resting gently on his shoulder, almost nodding off but still managing to look gorgeous.

Sam wonders what she is doing with him and how she has decided it is him she wants, rather than others who make unsuccessful and ill-timed bids for her attentions. Sam feels fleetingly sorry for them because he knows the pain of rejection, but then decides that in his new world, all is fair in love and war.

Early on, Sam confides to his sexy, loyal and well-balanced girlfriend about his 'free-floating' anxiety and the way he experiences unpleasant butterflies and a sinking feeling in the pit of his stomach. It is completely outside anything she has ever known or experienced because all the parts of her are properly integrated and she is naturally well-balanced without having to even think about it. She just *is*.

Sam discovers what he thinks he has already found out over the preceding months, which is that apart from her many other attributes, she is highly intelligent and someone who thinks, listens and reflects. She is very sweet about all that Sam tells her, and one day comes back on her racer and tells him that she has spotted a university counselling centre in town. Sam summons up all his courage and goes once or twice but it does no more than scratch the surface of what has taken over his life and he decides to simply carry on burying everything as he has done before.

There is an occasion when Chloe stays the night at Sam's parents' home. Marieke looks awkward but makes it clear when discussing sleeping arrangements that she thinks they ought not to be sleeping together. Chloe is aghast but swallows her surprise, smiles and, without missing a beat, tells Marieke that actually they are doing just that and that is exactly what will be happening tonight. Wonderful, balanced, courageous Chloe!

Again, Sam sees through the window which is ajar on his mother's past. Wayward, carnal father Aksel, who in Marieke's mind had her mother locked away for years before Kristina escaped and finally committed suicide, robbing Marieke of her mother and tainting her view of male sexuality for ever.

Somehow in Marieke's mind, Sam has become mixed up in all this, perhaps because he is the youngest. Perhaps little Sam's show of precocious virility in the bathroom all those years ago still snags painfully with the tangled strands of Marieke's precious memories of the mother she had taken from her as a child and all that preceded that devastating loss. Marieke does not wish Sam to become the sexual creature that created such emotional mayhem for her through her understanding of her own father's behaviour.

Further Up the Beach

Now though, she senses that she has met her match in Chloe. Marieke's view of the world can perhaps never be changed but its influence on Sam is now waning.

Sam ends his teaching year and goes on a camping holiday with Chloe's family. Her parents are libertarian in a way so far not known to Sam, and he and Chloe share their own little tent. Here, they do their best to meet the challenge of being surrounded only by canvas and awake to the sound of the gently gurgling sea and the enraptured squeals of small children who have escaped their night-time captivity.

Chloe now seems to see a long-term future with Sam, who seems relaxed and extrovert but has more hang-ups than he knows what to do with and no obvious means of sorting them out. His only plan remains to carry on burying everything deep, acting to the rest of the world as if he is extrovert and relaxed and hoping everything will turn out okay. He has told Chloe about his anxiety and she has seen him at his worst when he has sulked and ignored her for no good reason. But still Sam fears that she does not know most of it because there is so much more that he can neither articulate nor understand.

So Sam talks with her seriously and tells her that although he thinks she is great, he also knows deep down that he is seriously screwed up and that it is only fair that she knows that. Sam honestly does not know whether he is capable of bringing her the happiness she deserves. He is not consciously warning her off because he thinks himself undeserving of her – or perhaps he really is? He just wants her to know the truth and does not want to dupe her into believing him to be the relaxed, laid-back laugh he pretends to be most of the time. He wants her to be truly in the know about him.

She listens carefully and promises to give the whole thing some careful thought when she returns home. Then Sam will be spending a month abroad with children from the residential home where he has recently started to work, after he has discovered, as he is soon to do, what he should already have known: that he and teaching history do not go together.

Towards the end of Sam's time in France, a letter arrives from her and he retreats to a quiet spot to read it. She starts it, 'Dear Sammy', which has become Sam's sobriquet amongst her and her Oxford housemates. Then she says that she has thought very carefully about what he has told her and what she should do in the future. Sam's heart misses a beat and he rushes quickly to her conclusion and finds that she goes on to say that she is very clear in her own mind that no-one, including Sam, can persuade her that he should not continue to be her man.

Sam is touched to tears by her words but also scared that he will not be able to repay the faith she has shown in him. He is also aware that Chloe knows her own mind, and once it is made up, she is not easily swayed. He wishes he could share her confidence in himself but nevertheless is massively and deeply cheered. This irreverent, fun-loving girl with a remarkable head for figures has touched something deep in the core of his soul. She has told him that she believes in him. Now all Sam needs to do is believe in himself.

19. ON PROBATION

Sam soon realises that the history teaching idea is not only not a good one but actually an extremely bad one. Despite his degree and his attempts to mug up on the many centuries that are a blank to him, he remains sublimely ignorant of what a history teacher needs to know. He should never have followed in Charles's footsteps as he did, but to do otherwise was in his mind to risk not gaining the prize of parental approval he still craves.

So now Sam finds himself on teaching practice in a boys' public school because there is a policy of encouraging students to teach in a school completely different to that which they attended in their younger years. Sam is in an all-male environment and surrounded by established teachers in gowns and much pomp and formality. It is very different in every way to the radical comprehensive school he attended a few years ago.

Ironically, he is now closer to the kind of place which Walter always said he would like to send him to acquire polish and confidence, although Sam also knows that his father considers it to be one of those lesser 'tin pot' public schools, rather than the real deal he desperately hankered after for his children.

Now Sam stands in front of the class, supposed to be teaching about William Pitt, and is asked the most basic of questions about whether this is Pitt the Younger or Pitt the Elder. He does not have the foggiest clue, makes a blind guess and quickly realises from the look on the face of his supervisor who is observing the lesson, as well as those of some of the boys, that he has backed the wrong horse.

This is the moment of truth, the moment of humiliation when he realises that it is all over, the game is up and he has been found out, though of course there are already suspicions that he is masquerading as something he is not. Although Sam gets through the year, it is clear that history teaching is not for him and this hare-brained scheme needs to be revised.

There are, though, a couple of glimmers of hope.

The first is that Sam does not actually give a damn about being a history teacher and considers that he might just have been saved from a career he never would have wanted in the first place.

The other is just as important. Although most of the students are immensely privileged, there are some who struggle with school, relationships and the demands made upon them and he finds himself drawn to them because of his own pain. He senses that, despite the weight of what he has carried and continues to carry from his own past, he can help those struggling young people to overcome their difficulties. It is also clear that those who struggle on the margins of this elite establishment can both talk with Sam and trust him as someone who might be able to understand.

Further Up the Beach

So after Sam has got the piece of paper that tells him he is now a qualified teacher, he finds work for a few months in a children's home, where abuse, neglect and trauma have left their indelible marks on those for whom this is now home. A little later, he goes on to work with troubled youths, whose offending has brought them before the courts and who have also suffered as children at the hands of those whose job was to support, guide and nurture them but whose own childhood traumas still play havoc with their lives.

Before too long, Sam heads off to study for a qualification in social work. It is a great two years and he starts to feel that he is heading in the right direction. But he is brought up short when, towards the end of his time there, he sees a note on his personal file, written by the psychology lecturer who interviewed him at the start of the course. She comments that, in interview, Sam presented as someone who appears to have unresolved issues of identity and direction and suggests that this is something that could perhaps be addressed as part of the placement experience process.

When Sam spots this, he feels upset, angry and defensive about what he has chanced upon. This completely gets in the way of the possibility of him considering it in a way that might be helpful to him. It does not help that nobody raises it with Sam, and so nothing happens as a result. Perhaps it was meant to happen but did not because someone's courage failed them. But regardless, the priceless opportunity for Sam to trace and face this disappears until many years later.

After training, Sam arrives at his new inner city office as a qualified probation officer, feeling thrilled as he drives his little white Mini to report for his first day at work. He has always picked up on Walter's undisguised discontent about his own work in the business world, which he has always found mundane, compared to his halcyon days during the war. For his part, Sam desperately wants to be part of something else, not only to show his father how different he is to him but also to help other people in a way he feels he has not been helped himself.

His new work place is a great place to be. It is egalitarian in that the organisation's head and a brand new recruit like Sam both get the same generous holiday entitlement, and Sam and his colleagues all get to choose what colour they want their individual offices to be. It is brimming with energetic, idealistic young people wanting to make a difference, many of whom are, like Sam, rebels who strongly identify with those on their caseloads, despite also being officers of the court.

Sam builds up a caseload of many young black, disaffected teenagers, as well as old lags who have been round the system more times than anyone has cared to count.

At the end of the year, he is confirmed in post by Cecil, a senior manager whose practice days have been spent during the heyday of psychodynamic casework of the 1960s and 70s. He reads the report from Sam's manager, which is effusive about his abilities, and comments on Sam's well-balanced personality and his presentation as casual, relaxed and somewhat disarming. The disguise seems to be working! Cecil is positive too but maybe he sees or senses something else, using his finely-tuned psychodynamic antennae, commenting in conversation with Sam that 'only Sam knows what kind of man he goes to bed with'.

Afterwards, Sam plays this hilarious double entendre back to friends and colleagues and they all laugh like drains, as it confirms their view that it is high time the old codger is put out to grass. But Cecil is simply asking whether Sam is comfortable with the real Sam. Maybe Cecil says something similar to all such budding probation officers starting permanent employment or perhaps he has spotted a discrepancy within Sam. But Sam is not in any position to acknowledge what he might be getting at because he has too much invested in pretending to be who he is, and no-one else around him at the time is wanting to press the case and further explore Cecil's query.

A few of Sam's colleagues attend the whacky training course called 'Freeing yourself for the job', which Sam and most of his team believe belongs to a bygone age, as of course they are also convinced does psychodynamic Cecil. They avoid the course like the plague and decide conveniently that the world is made up of emotionally strong people on the one hand and others who are emotionally frail on the other. They formulate the view that anyone who is not up to the job emotionally should simply not be doing it and therefore there should be no need for any such courses which, rumour has it, can turn into much emotional blood-letting.

This protects Sam and others from looking at themselves and understanding that perhaps everyone is vulnerable in one way or another and there is no shame in that. However, nothing, absolutely nothing, will persuade Sam that this is the case.

He does some good work with complex and difficult people and feels a satisfaction that he is reaching out to enable them to acknowledge their pain, even though he can on no account remove the lid from his own. Sam is much more suited to this than to teaching history. But he is also aware that some of what the young men on his caseload tell him about their difficulties sparks something jarring and uncomfortable in him about his own.

Perhaps it is this which contributes to his free-floating anxiety becoming more acute and turning at times into fully-fledged panic attacks. It may also be a fear that, having finally arrived in a place he wants to be, Sam now runs the risk of it all collapsing around him if he were to let down his guard and dare to reveal that he is not quite the person he seems to be. Perhaps it is also because this is a difficult place to be a white man, with gender politics, rampant feminism and anti-racism finding their voice, making it even more difficult for Sam to find his own.

Now when Sam sits in team meetings, he sometimes experiences a sudden rush of adrenaline, which leads to him feeling panic-stricken and out of control. He is overwhelmed by something infinitely more powerful than himself, which threatens to smother the breath from his body and abandon him to a terrifying and ignominious end. As he struggles to find his breath as the meeting continues around him, he clings desperately to the handkerchief Walter taught him never to be without, praying that this will prove to be his saviour. Sam tries to believe each time will be the last, but the next is always lurking round the corner, ready to pounce suddenly and without mercy.

He confides only in Chloe, who is now his wife. She continues to believe in him and does all she can to support him. Sam goes through agonies of endlessly reliving the moments when things have gone wrong, feeling angry and diminished that he can neither control nor understand them and dreading when the next one might happen.

Further Up the Beach

Sam and Chloe visit Marieke and Walter regularly. By now Walter's fragmented nerves and resulting erraticism are compounded by the vivid spectre of his fast-accelerating demise, against which he fights with every ounce of his fading strength. Sam, on the other hand, is proud that he is now a working man and has evidence that others value him, whatever the struggles for him in keeping the lid on everything bubbling beneath the surface.

On one visit, he shows one of his very positive appraisals to his parents to give them an idea of what he is doing and who he has become. Walter reads it and comments angrily that such overstatement of someone's abilities is not helpful to the person concerned and in any case cannot possibly be true.

On another occasion soon afterwards, they are having a meal with Marieke and Walter. Sam gives them the flavour of court that morning, which includes his picking up the consequences of a sad and wretched drug-addicted prostitute who has appeared in court and has several children needing care. Walter's switch flicks immediately and dramatically and he starts to rant and rave that the state is supporting a drug addict and challenges Sam aggressively as to why that should be the case. Sam ends up feeling responsible for this situation and defends it with all his might against the intensity of his father's naked rage. Marieke also wants Sam to answer these charges, leading Sam to feel he has made a terrible mistake in seeking to share with his parents something of what he has become.

A little while later, Sam drops in with Chloe to see his parents, acutely aware of their need for support in the face of Walter's declining health. Almost before they have said hello,

Walter goes absolutely berserk when he sets eyes on Sam and sees that he has not shaved for a day or so and has stubble on his chin. Sam probably also looks scruffy and almost certainly has much longer hair than Walter would like.

This reminds Sam of his father's reaction to *Top of the Pops* a few years ago and he wonders whether Walter is going to have another heart attack. Though Sam thinks he knows his father well, he is nevertheless poleaxed by his reaction and leaves feeling deeply upset and angry. He stays away for a while, hoping Walter might ring to apologise, but the phone stays silent and unforgiving.

When Sam relents and goes to visit again, Walter makes no reference to his previous visit. Instead, he tells Sam crisply that he and Marieke are entertaining business guests for dinner in the near future. He makes sure Sam knows the date and then goes on to explain that he does not wish Sam to be seen at home when this happens. On no account does Walter wish his youngest son to meet his business guests.

It is at this point that Sam truly realises what he has suspected for many years but tried not to believe. Not only does Walter seem not to understand anything about who Sam is or what he has decided to do. Not only does he continue to seek to control Sam as he did when he was a child, on occasions stepping this up to the war footing recalled so vividly by Walter from his Air Force days. Now he has made it crystal clear that he is actually actively ashamed of Sam and the person he has become. He has given up on all attempts to shape Sam in the image of his own choosing and has thrown in the towel.

Meanwhile, at work, Sam is a rising star and he is promoted to a management role much more quickly than most. This means that he earns more money now and is also able to put a very convenient buffer between his own unresolved emotional pain and that of his clients because now he is expected to manage the team, rather than continue with face-to-face work.

He calls Marieke and Walter urgently to tell them the news. Walter is on good form and congratulates Sam, saying that being a probation officer is one thing but being a 'gaffer' is quite another. Sam dares not believe that perhaps he has now turned the corner and gained his father's approval at last.

But within a year, Walter is dead. His body turns to ashes at the crematorium on the same day as do all the screeds Sam has written about him and their relationship, as he puts a match to the incinerator in their tiny suburban garden.

Sam dares to hope that the end of Walter's life will also mean the end of what has plagued him for as long as he can remember. He keeps the card from the florist saying 'In Loving Memory of Dear Dad' in his wallet, which he carries at all times in his inside jacket pocket, close to his own heart. Sam looks forward to the future, sad and scarred, but also optimistic that this really might be a new beginning.

20. BOOMERANG

Years turn into decades, and slowly Sam successfully puts more distance between his troubled past and those of his clients. He becomes professionally successful, speaks at conferences and even appears several times on television. He loves and needs all this because it is a shortcut to boosting his own very fragile sense of self, although the adrenaline rush always quickly wears off and when he comes down to earth again, he finds that he is Sam, just Sam again.

Together he and Chloe raise their wonderful children Barnaby, Oliver and Poppy. Sam is thrilled that he is now building his own family. He wonders what he will be like as a father as he recalls his own childhood experiences, but somehow, with Chloe's help, he finds it deep within him to become a loving father without the hectoring and erratic inconsistencies he experienced as a child.

He worries that all this might deteriorate, even crumble, as he becomes old and grumpy and his tiny children become adolescents and eventually adults, but it does not and they stay very close, connected and with anything but rancour.

They move house several times over the years, eventually buying a wreck of a place which is neither terraced nor semi-detached, but detached, like the house Sam grew up in. Perhaps it is simply not possible to be a child of Sam's own family without that aspiration.

But the thrum of anxiety almost never leaves Sam, other than when he is at home with his family and when he sleeps at night. It is in his heart, it is in his head and it is in his bones, however much he tries to keep it at bay through the latest relaxation techniques he has learnt. He detests this ever-present foe and even more so himself for its domination of his soul. But it is like the woolyafus that attached itself so firmly to the trees all those years ago and has the silent, unerring determination of the thousands of red ants he recalls so vividly from his early childhood. Sam is also terrified of its immense power to flourish whatever the circumstances and can see no way in the world of escaping its malevolent power.

This is still absolutely top secret and shared only with Chloe, who has now successfully built her own thriving home-based accountancy business, always making short work of solving the financial dilemmas of her grateful clients. But the challenges Sam faces and shares with her are not so easily resolved. Chloe listens intently to all that Sam has to tell her, but though eternally patient, is also powerless.

Sam regularly redoubles his efforts at disguise, and for the most part, these are successful and he is regarded as good fun, extrovert and someone whose good humour shines through in most situations. He does lots of different jobs at work and hopes that each one will enable him to leave the old Sam behind. But it always catches up with him soon afterwards. At home, he hops from one DIY project to another, partly because they need doing but also because they provide a welcome distraction for Sam and the person he is struggling to escape from, or perhaps the person he is struggling to become.

When at various times he has flashes of realisation that this is not working, he tries acupuncture, hypnotherapy and homeopathy, each time daring to hope that one will provide the answer. But they only scratch the surface and he concludes reluctantly that what he experiences day to day is not only mysterious but also completely insoluble.

As Sam's own family grows, so the one in which he grew up changes shape and implodes before his eyes. His brother and sisters all live within the shadow of Walter's life and death and, though he means different things to each of his children, they cannot escape him.

With only Marieke left to glue together the disparate parts of the family, it fractures, and the siblings, now freed from the pressures of childhood familial perfection and with partners and children of their own, fall out dramatically. Their differences are not simply those of opinion, but instead at times seem to be elemental fights for power, supremacy and control.

When Marieke dies many years after Walter, the scene is set for the battle as to the form her funeral should take and who should lead on what, with only Joy maintaining a sense of balance and equilibrium. Charles's coronation as king, following Walter's death almost two decades before, still evokes bitter and lingering resentment, and this time, the siblings will not so easily be denied the final opportunity to take the lead and seek to tell everyone else what to do.

Throughout these times and beyond, Sam stays close to his beloved twin sister Joy but develops a separate existence in a way which was difficult for him during childhood.

He and Charles are at loggerheads for many years, during which Sam is sure that he is right and his older brother is wrong. Their relationship triggers in Sam painful memories of that with his father, and conflict sometimes seems to be almost inevitable.

However, at last, perhaps aware of their own mortality, the brothers rally and re-establish their relationship through regular meetings. Although different in every conceivable way, Sam and Charles have succeeded nevertheless in salvaging something highly valued and vital to them both and are perhaps even on a journey of discovery that blood is thicker than water, after all.

But Helen's sudden decision to move to the remotest Scottish island, where there is said to be no mobile phone coverage and whose post office is located in a converted shed, seems to set the seal on the dislocation between Sam and his older sister. Here she seeks her peace, just as her siblings must seek their own, though Sam will never believe that there may not be a way back for he and Helen to mend their relationship before the process of ossification is complete.

Sam goes through a severe midlife crisis which leads him to behave in a way which he should not, at a point in his life when he would like to be content but is struggling to be so. At around the same time, he becomes intensely and absurdly preoccupied by his previous love for holy Hattie. She returns to his thoughts and dreams in the most vivid form imaginable, sometimes smiling that scintillating smile

Further Up the Beach

which makes his heart leap and at other times looking at him reproachfully with her twinkling blue eyes.

Sam again experiences the intense joy of his unbridled love for Hattie, as well as the acute pain of rejection back in the year Red Rum romped home to victory and Joan Armatrading's 'Love and Affection' blasted from the bedrooms of their shared northern university campus. Sam's red-hot passion burned for Hattie, set against her ice-cool reason and false virtue; his pure, naked, vindictive love for her set against her affection for him; her beautiful Home-Counties accent set against his own which marked him as nothing but a Midlands' boy; her demure loveliness set against his clumsy ill-at-ease gawkiness.

Seeking to relive all this after more than 30 years, and aching most of all to hear once more that voice of southern symphonic beauty, makes perfect sense to Sam but cannot be explained rationally because, of course, life has moved on and such things simply can never, nor should ever, be.

All this remains unknown to Chloe, but having thoroughly tested the depth of her love for him, Sam thinks he is over the hump of what made him go off the rails. She has been magnificent in continuing to love Sam throughout the dark days of his introspection. But he does not arrive at the next decisive point until, in middle age, he and Chloe holiday on their own in France.

They have just arrived at their gîte and are in that carefree holiday mood when nothing matters and life seems rich. Sam has a sudden urge to pose nude at the top of the wooden stairs and have his holiday photo taken. Chloe, his wonderful Chloe, who always teases him about being a Narcissus, reluctantly agrees.

Sam stands smiling at the camera, one foot on the ground, the other on a shelf next to the stairs, even hamming it up a bit for dramatic effect. His cock is loose and flaccid, but by the time the shutter clicks, it has started to grow erect. He studies the resulting image with a mixture of surprise, maybe disbelief, and even admiration. He briefly questions whether this is in fact him and whether there has been some mistake, but equally he knows that what he sees is incontrovertible. He is not only present, he has a presence which is tangible, corporeal and irrefutable. What Sam sees is an apparently confident and crisply-delineated man. He looks good!

Sam's unique self is set before him; it is him, and yet whilst he recognises this to be the case, at the same time there is a part of him that can hardly believe the evidence before his own eyes. He is shown to be a separate person in his own right. He takes on a form of which he need not only be unashamed but can be proud. His own self is beyond doubt separate from that of his twin sister with whom his identity has at times been blurred.

In Walter's urgent need to throw Sam further up the beach, he may have hectored, even been ashamed of Sam and unwittingly eroded his sense of self, but no-one can take away the evidence Sam now sees before his own eyes.

Ralph Ellison, author of *Invisible Man*, wrote in the post-war years of his struggles to acquire that which lives within others from the moment of their birth: an understanding, at last, that he is in fact nobody but himself. Sam reads this and has the eerie but wonderful feeling that he is not alone.

Enter Sam; at last.

21. SEA BED

As middle age progresses, Sam realises things are careering out of control. He also senses a vital staging post in his life and knows there is a nettle he must grasp if things are ever to change. At this point, Sam is already older than his father when Walter was carried downstairs on a stretcher in the family's new home with his massive coronary, and not so many years younger than Walter when he died.

Sam knows that, while there is still time, it is also running away from him and will soon be gone. Although he has spent many years running for cover and is scared, even petrified, at the prospect of finding out more, at the same time he is intensely curious.

A few sessions of highly popular cognitive behavioural therapy briefly tempt Sam, but he decides that his needs are greater, and now is, purely and simply, make or break time. This is the time to test Freud's stated ambition of replacing neurotic unhappiness with ordinary unhappiness, if unhappiness of any sort there must be. So eventually, he calls a psychoanalytic psychotherapist, which sounds about right to Sam. He is not simply seeking the opportunity to talk about all that is going on in his mind to bring short-term relief, but also he must now embrace and understand his tireless tormentor.

He tells the therapist a bit about himself and she suggests an exploratory session to assess whether anything might be gained from him engaging in therapy with her. They agree a time to meet but then she wants to know Sam's name and address so that she can write to him confirming the appointment. She must also, of course, know the identity of the person who is walking into her consulting rooms.

Sam hesitates, stumbles and prevaricates, eventually saying he would prefer not to tell her, such is his sense of secrecy in harbouring what he considers to be this most shameful need. She, however, is firm and unequivocal – if he is to proceed with the appointment, she needs to know who he is. Even more important, she tells him that if he chooses not to tell her this, it is likely that his resolve will weaken, the appointment will not happen and the opportunity will be missed – in short, Sam will 'go underground' again.

So reluctantly, very reluctantly, Sam provides his name and address, and in doing so, takes the first step towards climbing the mountain which looms large and forbidding in front of him.

Therapy for Sam shares similar feelings of terror and exhilaration with parachuting, but at times is much scarier. He lies week after week on the couch, at first feeling odd, awkward, embarrassed and thoroughly exposed. He witnesses many repeats of the seasons from this vantage point and observes that in winter, the lamp in the corner casts a shadow of a beautifully proportioned pair of breasts on the wall above, something he only notices and comments on towards the end of his time there.

Over time, this space becomes his psychic home and he tells this stranger everything and every thought which has ever been in his head, as well as those he has dreaded and still dreads to have. He tells her about all the things that terrified him as a tiny boy and the thoughts and behaviours that have continued to tyrannise him as an adult.

Together they look down the telescope of Sam's life and the lives of his parents, always with the intention of understanding and illuminating, rather than apportioning blame or wrongdoing. Sam's father, who has been dead for more than 20 years but for whom Sam still feels such unresolved love and hatred, comes alive again, as does Marieke, following her death several years before.

All Sam's siblings take their places in the room at times too and his therapist looks patiently and enquiringly at the many family photos Sam brings to sessions, including those of him and Joy holding hands as young children, wearing clothes with the same pattern made by Marieke on her old Singer sewing machine, as well as those of Hattie and, of course, Chloe.

Sam reads lots and absorbs himself in deep reflection, at times wallowing deliciously in the lugubrious introspection of Howard Jacobson's novels and at others in the music of his teenage heroes Neil Young and Cat Stevens. He discovers, belatedly but gloriously, the depths and brilliance of the real master of poetry and introspection, Leonard Cohen, whom he sees in concert just at the moment when much of this is emerging through therapy for the first time. All this blasts through Sam's house at maximum volume and he feels a sense of ironic satisfaction that their detached home means that the neighbours will not be disturbed by this noisy, regressive, ageing hippie.

Amidst all this, he tastes again and savours the many positive childhood memories etched deep in his consciousness. That of being rescued by his father from Cub camp to watch England beat West Germany in 1966, the series of bikes Walter lovingly provided and maintained, those amazing Bonfire Nights he orchestrated and the summer holidays Sam could not wait to begin and prayed would never end.

Despite these, the overwhelming double well of shame into which he has fallen comes into sharper focus, Sam having unwittingly taken on responsibility for the deep shame felt by Walter about his inferiority amongst the officer class, as well as that which haunted Marieke in relation to the loss of her mother and the potential destructiveness of male sexuality.

It is a massive leap for Sam to understand that his mother's influence on his life was far more complicated than he has ever realised. Though Marieke can never be anything other than the dearest mother to Sam, it remains a challenge to understand how even this bold and plucky woman seemed powerless to protect him from the full force of his father's dire warnings of future failure and social shame, as well as his tirades against 1960s' youth culture and permissiveness.

Did Marieke perhaps struggle to recognise the man she had fallen in love with and married 20 years before?

Could it be that, despite her indomitable spirit and continental candour, she too was unsettled and even intimidated by the man Walter had become?

Further Up the Beach

Did Marieke also have to learn Walter's rules about social etiquette in the class-ridden post-war England she made her home? If so, this perhaps reveals something of the crushing weight borne by Walter in relation to these convictions and the extent to which he himself was a victim of their cruel and ceaseless oppression.

Sam also becomes aware of how desperately he had needed his father or brother to provide him with a source of emotional male intimacy to counteract the formidable power and influence of the female trinity of twin sister, elder sister and mother, amongst whom his own self was so compromised. But, through no fault of their own, neither Walter nor Charles had been able to offer Sam this gift, and in the process, help him connect with the person he was, which meant that he had come to fear these most fundamental parts of his own identity.

It becomes clear to Sam that, in order to free himself from the need for ever more imaginative self-punishment and loathing, he must allow himself to shed the dead weight of sadness and shame carried so bravely by Walter and Marieke for which he has somehow contrived to take responsibility. This can certainly never have been intended by his parents because, despite everything, Sam retains a clear and unmistakable sense that he was loved and cherished.

The shame, though, is no longer his responsibility to bear and he must learn to live without its perverse attraction and constant oppression. It is now time to 'step away from the cross' and his own irresistible urge towards self-sacrifice and incessant martyrdom. Nor is it any longer necessary for Sam to harbour the secret of his anxiety, which over the years has become every bit as shameful as shame itself.

He can now also cast off that crown of thorns he has created from the vestiges of his old relationship with Hattie, whose strict, anachronistic moral code only reinforced the messages of his childhood, leaving him in a turmoil of repressed pain which lingered for many decades. Sam may continue to be able to see and touch his youth as if it were still part of him but now he must embrace the reality of its irrevocable passing.

He must also recognise his vivid memories of Hattie's extraordinary perfection as a figment of his own imagination, created by the allure of the perfect outer shell his father so passionately desired for his youngest son, and for which Sam searched so long and hard.

Alongside this, the very many habits and rituals which have grown up with Sam to help protect him against all this are no longer needed. He can relinquish his anxiety and all that has developed around it, although this is a challenge because, though now redundant, this is almost as old as him and sometimes feels inseparable from him and his essence. He is getting to be an old dog but now, at last, new ways of thinking, being and behaving become possible.

He develops a blissful sense of his own whole self, which in turn creates an ease and comfort in his own skin which has been so elusive since his earliest memories of existence in the world. Clearing the multitude of tangled knots which have gone before, Sam starts to see more clearly his own unique self, his many strengths and the countless positives in his life.

He even starts, tentatively at first, to do the unthinkable and tip his winter soup towards him, as Walter warned so urgently against, wondering as he becomes bolder what

Further Up the Beach

his father might make of such insubordination. He recalls Walter's insistence that he must always carry a handkerchief and how consequently throughout his whole life it has always felt desperately unsafe to go anywhere without one. He will never forget the times when he rushed to work and discovered, panic-stricken, that he was without this essential piece of cloth, choosing to go out of his way to buy one rather than risk being without for the rest of the day.

The many handkerchiefs he has accumulated over the years, a mixture of plain, striped, spotty and checked, for so long the key to Sam's survival, now lie as relics of the past in a dusty old drawer, unaware of why they have been discarded or of the potent symbols of survival they once represented to their owner.

Sam must also face some of the less lovely bits about himself he would like to change, of which he has scarcely been aware and which are inextricably linked with the defences he has constructed over the decades. Like struggling with authority figures, having had such negative experiences of this as a child. Or withdrawing when he is with the one he loves but is feeling unloved and insecure, as he felt in his desperation for Walter's love, approval and intimacy which he so rarely glimpsed behind his father's expert disguise.

And though excessive form and formality will always fill Sam with detestation, loathing and fear because this represents the world in which he is most likely to be shamed and humiliated, he must recognise that there is sometimes a place for this and that he can remain safe and secure.

Now all this is in the open and understood, Sam decides to celebrate by casting off several decades as a manager to work again on the front line with young people, helping them dare to connect with the things they may not even know they feel and fear. His friends tell him he is mad, but he returns to learn the ropes, firstly in probation, which sadly has continued its journey into narrow, blinkered, adult-focused correctionalism, then with young people in trouble whose lives are blighted by their own negative childhood experiences, and finally with families experiencing multiple difficulties and struggling to find ways of resolving conflict and living together.

As he embarks on this journey a second time, Sam wonders how things might have been different for his family if his parents had only been able to talk about the earlier traumas in their lives, rather than being expected to show the stiff upper lip of their time. Or if he had been able to do the unthinkable and share what was going on inside his own head with an adult outside his close-knit family, which chose to isolate itself from those living around it and in which so much was reverberating painfully beneath the surface.

He wobbles briefly in his new practitioner role in using and mastering the necessary computer skills which are now an integral part of the job. But overwhelmingly, Sam now finds himself gloriously free of that toxic emotional contamination from his own past and so can now hear the pain and distress of others and help them in a way which was not possible as a young man. Not only has therapy taken him back to the earliest roots of his own existence in the world, but he is also now able to return to those professional roots from which he escaped so readily into management as an ambitious young man, driven and desperate for the ever-elusive approval of his father.

Further Up the Beach

As well as relinquishing his anxiety, so too after several years must Sam say goodbye to his therapist. She has been with him through the pain and exultation of discovery not only of his childhood and adolescence, but also as he journeyed into his parents' complex past, as well as Kristina's tragic history and all that this meant for Marieke and her relationship with her youngest son.

In many ways, it would be easier to continue the therapeutic journey, but he knows deep down that she has helped him do what he needed to do but doubted was possible when they first met. Sam asks her directly whether she believes he is ready to end their work together. Rather than throw this question back to him, as is her stock-in-trade, she replies that they both know the answer to this. The answer is 'yes'. Now she too has believed in Sam.

Finally, Sam celebrates the loyal, sexy and wonderful Chloe. She has chosen to stick with him through thick and thin, allowing him time and space for his mid-life perplexity, born of long-suppressed childhood demons hiding cannily in the darkest crevices of an anguished mind.

Now he understands, almost too late, the honour and responsibility he carries for Chloe's future happiness which she entrusted to him all those years ago in deciding that she believed in him. Chloe has given Sam their three wonderful children who are his inspiration and hope for the future, proof that one generation's pain need not infect the next.

***

It is summer time again and Sam drinks up the warmth of the sun and reflects that, in the unlikely event that he were ever to turn religious, there could be no finer object for veneration. This holiday, they are touring Anglesey, then heading across the Irish Sea to Dublin to stay in south-west Ireland. The day is fast approaching when Walter will have been dead for exactly 30 years and Sam has been wondering for many months how he might mark that event, as he will not be at home to visit the crematorium.

He goes to the tiny supermarket in Moelfre and searches the shelves, eventually finding just what he is looking for: a sturdy, attractive, small hexagonal jar with a decent waterproof lid. Its contents are not important but he notes with extra satisfaction that they are lemon curd, which sparks a powerful positive childhood memory of bread and butter evening teas. He takes the jar back to their holiday home, has his first taste of lemon curd for close to 50 years and then empties its remaining contents down the sink. He wonders whether this might create a blockage in their holiday home, so washes it down with piping hot water, just in case. Then he carefully soaks off the label before washing and drying the jar inside and out until it sparkles.

Then Sam heads down to the pebbled beach, overlooked by the lifeboat station, and the pub where he and Chloe have enjoyed evening meals throughout their stay. It is early evening, with clouds scudding across the sky, the sound of gulls and a rough sea filling the air and just a single solitary figure, Sam, sitting on the beach.

He searches carefully for six small attractive pebbles and, after agonising over endless possibilities, places his chosen few on one side, sitting these on his flip-flop to avoid them becoming lost amongst the many. Next, he reaches into his pocket to find his favourite handkerchief which is bright blue and checked and has been freshly washed and ironed for this most important of occasions. He places the handkerchief inside the jar to form a kind of lining and then puts the pebbles carefully inside, one for each member of the family he grew up in: one is Walter, one Marieke, one Charles, one Helen, one Joy and one him.

The pebbles are all of similar size but unique in shape, colour and texture, with none more important or dominating the others. They cluster together, close, snug and at ease with the differences each brings to their new home.

Sam brings the corners of the handkerchief together and ties a rudimentary knot to keep the contents safe, cushioned and comfortable. He finds a piece of decorative dried seaweed and places it on the top, before reaching inside his wallet and finding the card from the florist which he has carried round since his father's death and which says simply, 'In Loving Memory of Dear Dad'. Sam places this carefully next to the glass so that it can be easily seen and read. Then he screws the top up as tightly as he dares and carries his precious creation back to their cottage.

The following day, the thirtieth anniversary of Walter's death, he and Chloe are aboard the ferry which slowly sets out westwards from Holyhead, carefully picking its way out from the port towards the open sea. Sam goes out on deck, with his jar and its new and vital contents firmly zipped inside his fleece pocket.

He hopes he passes for some middle-aged or even perhaps elderly bloke who is determined to take the air, rather than giving away his true purpose. He looks out from the port deck and sees they are heading out parallel to land. Sam needs open sea and so swaps sides and waits a few minutes until mums and dads with small excited children have decided it is getting too cold and go back inside for warmth.

He is reminded of the family's first trip to Denmark in the 1960s and of the wild excitement he felt, along with a sense of disbelief that anything carrying cars could possibly float. He recalls separate precious family photos, one of all the family on a windy deck and the other just Walter also on deck, sporting a blazer and tie and looking grim and resolute – an Englishman abroad and a most reluctant one at that.

Now Sam is alone and gazing out to open sea as the ferry picks up speed, moving westwards out of Holyhead Bay and towards the Irish Sea. He takes out the jar and examines the contents one last time, feeling good about what he has created and sparking vivid memories of his father's life and death and all that he has experienced as a child and young man. He kisses it slowly and deliberately, thinking about what it now contains and the immensity of all that this means to him but which has been so hard to unearth. He debates whether his throw should be overarm or underarm in order to get it to a point as far away from the ferry as possible.

In the end, he plumps for a powerful backhand underarm throw, and watches with satisfaction as the jar and all he must bury makes a long and graceful arc before landing in its new home. The pebbles should pull it to the sea bed in no time at all, and Sam has high hopes of the strength of that chunky glass in helping it to withstand whatever challenges it might meet on its journey to its resting place. It bobbles briefly on the waves and almost immediately disappears from view.

Further Up the Beach

Sam stays looking out to sea for a few more minutes, thinking deep, reflective, cosmic thoughts. Then he returns to the warmth of the boat, looking very much the same as when he left a few minutes ago, though now more windswept, with a spring in his step and feeling different deep inside.

22. EPILOGUE

This is the brief story of Sam's illness, how he falls dramatically off the edge, though a different precipice from that which greeted his father at a similar age. Different also from that which greets those for whom the primary focus is emotional or mental ill health, but with which we all know the links are drawn tightly because of the inseparability of body and mind.

He knows in his heart of hearts that, although bad luck plays its part, so too does the culmination of his having been running to catch up ever since he can remember, always extending himself way beyond any kind of sensible limits in a misplaced bid to prevent his own imminent defeat, shame and annihilation.

Only a few days before this happens, Sam has said goodbye to his therapist, feeling a genuine and well-grounded ease about doing so and a sense that their work together is complete. During this time, they have left not a single pebble on the beach unturned. He leaves, feeling not only able to understand the underlying motivations for his deepest feelings and resulting behaviour but also having learnt to take responsibility for all this, as well as for the other less lovely parts of himself which are a greater part of the whole than he would wish them to be.

The night before Sam's dramatic collapse and hospitalisation, they are at a family party. Sam is caught alone on camera at the very end of the evening by the ever-wonderful Beryl, Chloe's mother, who tells Sam that he is the only one of the party she has not captured on film. He looks mellow, pissed and thoroughly content, which indeed he is at that moment, surrounded by his own adored family and others he loves so dearly.

Now Sam lies in his hospital bed, unable to sleep because of his own pain and because of the groans and urgent cries of those who fear they have been abandoned in their hour of need by nurses who, though magnificent, often look shattered and are rushed off their feet. Worse still, next to Sam is a confused elderly man who is reliving the trauma of having lost his entire family in concentration camps in Germany during the Second World War, his own life only having been saved on account of his being the youngest.

Lukasz's pain is magnified because he cannot make others understand much of what he is trying to say, nor understand why he needs to be confined in this alien environment at this advanced stage of his life. He wanders noisily into Sam's own private space in the middle of the night and tests Sam's compassion because he himself is feeling so very vulnerable and knows that, although his own experience can never compare with this tragic old man's, he must also look after himself and his future.

Further Up the Beach

As Lukasz is persuaded reluctantly to return to his own bed, Sam drifts into a disturbed, morphine-induced sleep in which he dreams that his hospital neighbour and his own father meet and exchange emotional stories of their involvement in the war. Sam is a bystander and watches transfixed as Walter comes alive again and the two men swap accounts of the life-changing conflict in which they played their unique parts.

As they hug in comradeship, Sam moves from observer to participant and enjoys the warm embrace of both men who celebrate Sam's existence and toast his future health and happiness with shots they each down in one gulp. Walter gazes intently into the eyes of his youngest son, then places his hand over Sam's and holds him tight, as he did when Sam was a young boy. Sam registers sublime delight at his father's loving gaze, and surprise at the firmness of his grip.

Then his father's face slowly fades, to be replaced by that of the night nurse bending over Sam to insert a new cannula in the back of his hand, so that his vital drip can continue uninterrupted throughout the rest of the night. Only Lukasz next door remains, recalcitrant and rejecting to all those who try to help and lost in the depths of his boundless sorrow.

During visiting hours, the mood of the ward changes to one of forced jollity. Sam feels so ghastly that he cannot face seeing many visitors. But his family comes and joins the party mood, bringing with them their love, as well as grapes and good wishes.

Barnaby and Oliver are now fine young men who remain the closest of friends, though now with their own careers and lovers. The brothers talk easily about their feelings but at the same time get on with their busy lives without undue angst. Poppy, an unexpected but treasured afterthought, now stands sleek, dark and feline-like in her prettiness, almost as tall as her mother, thanks to a self-willed late teenage growth spurt.

As Sam chats to them, propped up on ample institutional pillows, he is reminded of his final conversation with his own father as Walter's life ebbed away in hospital and Sam dared to hope that his father's death might bring him the relief he longed for. He feels confident that his own children are not feeling similarly, and so concludes that things have changed much for the better across the generations and that he has played his own unique part in this.

Chloe does her determined best to cheer Sam up with the daily crossword and his mind is cast back to memories of Marieke and their struggles with her crossword in her last years, months and days, helping them pass their evenings together and taking their minds off his mother's slow but certain decline.

As Joy strides in to the ward one evening to visit with Edward, her adored and adoring husband of many years, Sam has a fleeting but powerful image of his twin sister as a little girl on the first day of school when she acted as his intrepid protector in a hostile environment, as well as somehow finding the strength to look after herself. She too is a proud parent now, with childhood memories of her own, but shares many of Sam's early recollections of the complicated family of which they were a part and the death of their own father in similar surroundings all those years ago.

After many long nights in hospital, Sam is discharged, desperate to be away from the confines of hospital life and to be looked after at home. But here too, he still feels like a caged animal, and as a result becomes impossibly difficult to live with, his adrenaline following near-death still running high and powerful long-term drugs also playing their part. The trauma has been just as difficult, albeit in a different way, for poor Chloe as it has been for Sam, and at times they find it difficult to find their equilibrium in view of all that has happened. Sometimes scratchiness, bickering and frustration on both their parts do battle with harmony, consensus and forbearance, which they both find disconcerting.

But slowly things settle and Sam finds peace in being the individual he has struggled to be in the past, as well as in celebrating the relationship with himself which has been so elusive since his earliest childhood and which his therapist has helped him to uncover. He learns to cook and quickly becomes practised, confident and moderately adept at it. He absorbs himself in novels which he has often not had the time to do, and also takes an interest in what is going on in the world around him in a way he has only previously gone through the motions of doing.

Then his preoccupation with his own survival diminishes to allow the rebuilding of his relationship with Chloe, and together they reach heights of mutual understanding, compassion and sometimes even hilarity which surpass even the best times they have ever known. With Chloe's help, Sam also begins to look at and truly understand the magic of what is occurring in their lovely garden, rather than seeing it and it meaning next to nothing. Together they plan their future and even agree to one day get the dog they have so often dreamed of and which Poppy is adamant she can simply not live without.

David Monk

As Sam's recovery eventually allows these two old-timers to renew their love life, Sam listens again to Steve Miller's 'Fly Like an Eagle' and recalls the fun he and Chloe had in the old Minis all those years ago. They say that stiffness passes to the joints as we get older, and Sam has difficulty in conceiving how he might now even enter or exit an old-style Mini, much less do anything of note once inside.

It is now many years since mould on the old gnarled trees and dried peas caught hold in tiny Sam's vivid imagination and that army of red ants marched so terrifyingly into his childhood consciousness. The ghosts of the past deserve to be heard, and have had their say. They will never disappear, and may even shake and stir themselves from time to time, causing distant rumbles from a time gone by. But now the once all-powerful red army has been conquered and lies in tatters. Freedom, decides Sam as he surveys the future and wishing only that there could be more of it, tastes sweeter than he could ever have imagined.

Lightning Source UK Ltd.
Milton Keynes UK
UKHW011817310120
357972UK00001B/21